Digby
C.E.

Penalty

D1510551

Also by Michael Hardcastle

Soccer Captain
One Good Horse
Puzzle

Penalty

MICHAEL HARDCASTLE

**A Dolphin
Paperback**

First published in Great Britain by Dent Children's Books in 1990
Paperback edition published in 1995
by Orion Children's Books
a division of Orion Publishing Group Ltd
Orion House
5 Upper St Martin's Lane
London WC2H 9EA

Second impression 1996
Third impression 1997

Copyright © Michael Hardcastle 1990
Cover illustration © Neil Reed 1990

The right of Michael Hardcastle to be identified
as the author of this work has been asserted.

All rights reserved. No part of this publication
may be reproduced, stored in a retrieval system,
or transmitted, in any form or by any means,
electronic, mechanical, photocopying, recording
or otherwise, without the prior permission of
Orion Children's Books.

A catalogue record for this book is available
from the British Library.
Printed in Great Britain by Clays Ltd, St Ives plc

ISBN 1 85881 218 6

One

As Adam Skipsea flung himself across the goal, the red-haired boy sidefooted the ball into the net off the inside of the far post. Jason positively yelped with glee and congratulated himself, hands clasped high above his head.

'You'd've been offside there,' Adam pointed out as he retrieved the ball from under the spare rigging. 'No ref. would have let that count.'

'You're only saying that, Adam, because you didn't stop it going in,' said Carl. He wished desperately that he'd been the one to put the ball in the net. So far he hadn't outwitted the goalkeeper once.

'Listen, you've got to play to the rules,' Adam told him, 'otherwise there's no point in playing any game. If there are no rules there'd be no fun in scoring a goal, would there? Come on, you have a shot.'

'All right, then, I'll score the next goal from outside the box,' promised Jason confidently, smoothing down his russet hair with his left hand as he spoke. It was a gesture he'd copied from one of his sporting heroes.

Jason wished they had a couple of other boys to join in their astonishing impromptu training session; astonishing because they couldn't really believe their luck that Adam Skipsea, City's latest goalkeeping discovery, had actually asked if he could play with them. Jason and his pal Carl were simply kicking a ball fairly aimlessly into the goals on the youth club pitch at Riverside. They'd recognised Adam as soon as he jogged into view down Endless Bank. Only two days earlier they'd watched him in action for City in the home game with Everton. Now the two ten-year-olds were thrilled to be playing with their hero. For once, they couldn't wait for school on Monday – just to tell everyone.

Adam had been featured in the *Evening Mail* only the previous night: the paper had printed a whole sequence of his saves and clearances. It was, as the match reporter expressed it, 'a brilliant debut by a fearless and talented player. City have found a young goalkeeper of real star quality.' And now, in the midst of such glory, here he was, apparently quite happy to kick a ball about with two schoolboys he'd never met before.

'I'll give you a prize if you can score from that range,' Adam called out as Jason retreated to the very edge of the box. Jason sensed he meant it; Adam Skipsea wouldn't allow himself to be beaten by any shot if he could possibly keep it out. So the prize would be genuine; it would be worth winning. Jason speculated on what it might be: a spare pair of goalkeeping gloves; a goalie's jersey; a signed photo (no, surely not, because almost anybody could get that from a player just by asking); a football? The prospect of winning such a prize was so exciting that he put everything he possessed into his shot. But he tried too hard, the ball flying wide of Adam's right-hand post. The goalkeeper didn't even have to catch it and so it was Carl who scurried away to collect the ball from behind the goal.

'Can I have another go, Adam?' Jason called out. 'I got my foot too much under the ball that time. Next time I'll be right on target. Promise!'

Adam seemed to be pondering and Jason was dismayed. 'I mean, you don't have to give me a prize if I score,' he offered, looking as cheerful as he could.

'It has to be the best goal *anyone* has ever scored against me, ever,' Adam stipulated. 'And I'm the judge!'

Jason's jaw dropped but determination was part of his character and even if he didn't score he'd tell everyone at school that Adam Skipsea had laid down impossible conditions. He felt that would prove that Adam rated him a terrific player. He knew he could always rely on Carl to back him up anyway. Jason had long believed he possessed the skills to take him to the top in football one day. But he still couldn't resist showing off: and that was why he needed Carl as an audience as well as a friend. Carl was sometimes embarrassed by Jason's boasting but, because of his own shyness, he rarely objected to it and never in front of other people.

Jason gestured to Carl to fire the ball at him from the edge of the box and to direct it in such a way that he could hit it on the volley with all the force he commanded. He decided to aim for the bottom right-hand corner of the net: a spot just inside the post. His soccer coach at the Sunday League club he played for always insisted that was the most difficult part of the target area for a goalie to cover. He would put Adam 'under maximum pressure', to borrow the coach's favourite expression. Carl, for once, got things absolutely right.

The ball bounced at exactly the right height as Jason ran on to it for a right-footed piledriver and his accuracy was at peak level. His shot was about to zip into the net, first bounce, when Adam just managed to smother the ball at the furthest extent of his reach. This time Jason flung his arms in the air in utter exasperation; it was perhaps as well his parents didn't hear the words he muttered because they'd never approved of even the mildest oath. A phrase like that would have cost Jason at least a week's pocket money. His only consolation was that Adam signalled, with a raised thumb, his approval of the quality of the shot.

Someone else who applauded, though in a somewhat mocking manner, was a man wearing a well-cut grey suit and a trilby hat in an unusual shade of blue. He'd just arrived on the scene, having reached the edge of the pitch by a route across the foot of Endless Bank that gave him a good view of what was happening.

'If you can save shots like that you ought to concentrate on playing with people of your own age,' the man told Adam. Adam just smiled and punted the ball back to the boys. He was used to spectators behind his goal making all sorts of remarks. It was usually best to ignore them. One or two had been deeply wounding, and obviously intended to provoke him or at the very least upset his concentration. Some succeeded. Adam hadn't yet learned to remain calm whatever the provocation. He frequently wanted to race behind the goal and thump the offender.

Jason, eager for another chance of a shot, was hovering by the penalty spot but Adam indicated that it was Carl's turn to have a go; and Carl's face immediately glowed with pleasure.

'Of course, you're just wasting your time,' remarked the spectator. 'Instead of bashing a bit of plastic around you ought to be getting your head down, studying for a proper job, planning a proper future for yourself. Too many people just collecting unemployment money these days.'

'I have planned my future,' Adam replied in a mild conversational tone. 'I'm already in City's first team and I'm going to play in goal for England. Yes, at this silly game – kicking a bit of plastic, catching it, keeping it out of the net.'

'What's your name, then, so I can see if you do get there?' the man asked.

'Adam Skipsea.'

'Skipsea? It's an unusual name.' Blue Hat frowned. 'Any relation to a young woman called Zoe Skipsea? Works at Seabright Villas, she does.'

Adam, fielding another shot from Jason, turned in surprise. 'That's my sister,' he said warmly. 'How do you know her? Have you got a relative who lives at the Villas?'

The frown was now a scowl. 'No, nothing like that. Just – idle curiosity, that's all. But I know her all right. Look, I've got to be going. Wasted enough time here as it is.'

On that sour note, Blue Hat hurriedly departed without so much as a backward glance. Adam would have liked to find out why the man had mentioned Zoe but he was distracted again by the boys.

Carl began to exchange short, sharp passes with Jason, now aware that it was up to him to get the ball past City's new star goalkeeper. Adam, however, sensed to the split-second when the boy was going to shoot. He had no difficulty in knocking the ball up as it reached him at chest height and then, spinning through three hundred degrees, catching it almost behind his back with one hand. He was showing off, which coaches always tell you never to do, but he didn't think the boys would mind: they'd expect something out of the ordinary from a professional player. That was how he'd been at their age, only a handful of years ago.

Adam punted the ball back to Jason and called: 'I think this'll have to be your last go. Got to go home and phone a mate about a car I'm thinking of getting.'

'Oh, Adam, don't go yet!' Jason agonized. 'We've got loads of time to play tonight. Can't you phone up later?'

Adam laughed. 'Look, I only stopped off for a couple of minutes, really. Told you, I was supposed to be on a training run. Professional footballers have to stick to a proper routine to keep fit, you know.'

Jason, who'd been bouncing the ball with neat control from one foot to the other, suddenly trapped it. 'Hey, what sort of car are you going to get?' he wanted to know.

'No idea,' Adam replied with a shrug. 'Anything that goes'll suit me. I think –'

'A BMW, that's what you want. Or no, maybe a Porsche!' Carl put in excitedly. 'They're terrific and the speed you can –'

'Hang on! I can't afford anything like that,' Adam laughed. He leaned back against one of the goalposts, arms folded across his chest. 'Footballers aren't all millionaires, whatever you read in the papers. Well, City's players aren't, anyway. A decent second-hand Ford will suit me, just as long as it's reliable.'

'No, no, you want something good now you're famous, Adam,' Carl pointed out, determined that City's goalkeeper should take the matter of his personal car seriously.

'Look, it's like I said, I can only have what I can afford.' Adam moved away from the post. 'Maybe later when –'

'Bet you can't get this one, Adam!' yelled Jason.

6

Disappointed by what he considered to be his new friend's imminent desertion, he fired in a well-aimed lob that was going to pass over the goalkeeper's head unless he took immediate action.

Instinctively, Adam jumped and succeeded in diverting the ball with the tips of his fingers; it rose vertically and he was able to collect it nonchalantly when it came down again.

'You were dead lucky there, Adam,' Jason scoffed. 'It was going right into the top corner. 'I'd've won a prize for that, no danger.'

'Adam didn't say he was giving a prize for any more goals, did you, Adam?' Carl said anxiously, suspecting that Jason was in danger of alienating their new hero. He hoped Adam might invite them to attend a match as his guests and that they would be allowed to see the changing-rooms and the communal bath and all the other fascinating places under the main grandstand, territory that was always out of bounds to the general public except on special occasions.

'Another time perhaps,' said Adam, drop-kicking the ball into the distance. 'It was a bit of fun, wasn't it, and even a work-out for me. Can't have enough of those, you know.'

Jason hared off to retrieve their ball before it could reach the river. Carl dropped into step beside Adam who was generous enough not to depart at top speed.

'Have you always been a goalkeeper, Adam?' he inquired earnestly. 'I mean, is that what you always wanted to be?'

Adam grinned, running his fingers through his thick, curly dark brown hair. 'That's what everybody asks, almost as if it's incredible for anyone to want to be a keeper. But, well, I didn't mind where I played as long as I got a game. Usually it's the smallest kid around who gets stuck in goal, isn't it, because no one else wants to play there. I wasn't the smallest but I wasn't all that tall, either. I shot up when I was about thirteen or fourteen. It just happened that I went in goal for one game and made a few fairly spectacular saves and decided I liked it. But when I got the chance I had a go at scoring goals, too. Even hit a hat-trick, once!'

'But you're going to stay a goalkeeper now, aren't you?'

'Oh, sure. I know now it's my best position. And I like the job, I really do. I want to be the best. As I told that guy who stopped to watch us, I intend to be right at the top one day.'

Jason, having dribbled the ball back at speed, rejoined them, eager to contribute to the conversation and further delay Adam's departure. 'D'you think you'll have to leave City, then, to get to the top?'

'Come off it! I've only just got into the first team!' Adam paused in astonishment at Jason's question. 'I didn't even expect that so soon. So what're you talking about, Jason?'

Inevitably, the auburn-haired, stockily-built boy had a ready answer. 'Oh, my dad says City have made a habit of letting their best players leave just when they need them to get to the top themselves. Says they just don't have enough ambition – City, I mean.'

Carl shot a worried glance at his friend, afraid that Adam would react angrily to such criticism. But Adam treated it quite matter-of-factly.

'Don't think that's true any more, even if it was once. Now we're in the First Division we intend to stay there. All the lads feel that way. The Boss – Ian Fenn – well, nobody could say he hasn't got plenty of ambition. Wouldn't be here otherwise. I reckon – the

Boss reckons – we've got a pretty good squad at present. Things are clicking. Could be we'll surprise a lot of the critics.'

'Hope so,' said Carl fervently. 'Hope you win the League and the Cup and – and everything else. Then I can tell everybody you came and trained with Jason and me, show 'em how you make your brilliant saves!'

Adam glanced down at him, noting the thin features and slim frame. 'Ever thought of keeping goal yourself, Carl?'

'Wouldn't mind, but I don't think I'll ever be big enough,' was the honest answer. 'I'm sure my hands won't be.'

'Hands don't have to be huge, you know. Mine certainly aren't. But your fingers do have to be, well, strong and supple. A keeper who kept breaking a finger stopping shots would be no good at all.'

'So have you never broken a finger, then?' Carl inquired in a serious tone.

'Not yet, thankfully, and touch wood,' laughed Adam, tapping his head jovially. 'If you do the right exercises and you train all the time I believe you can improve any skills and talents and even your bones. Anyway, I must dash.'

'If you come on another training run round here we could join in again, couldn't we?' asked Carl, now desperate to keep in touch. 'That'd be just great for us, honestly. We both want to be top players ourselves, don't we, Jason?'

'Spot on,' replied Jason, grinning at having thought of such a sophisticated expression.

'Well, I don't know just when I'll be coming this way again,' said Adam. 'I don't take this route daily, you know.'

'Well, I could give you a ring if you don't mind, and

tell you when we'll be here if you're coming this way,' Jason pressed eagerly. 'Then we could bring our autograph books – oh, and cameras so we could have pictures of ourselves with you. That'd be terrific. I mean, you're in our phone book, aren't you?'

'Er, yes, I am,' Adam conceded. He still lived with his parents and Skipsea was an unusual enough name for there to be only a handful of them in the telephone directory. 'But I'm not making any promises, understand?'

'Oh, sure. We won't expect any favours, Adam,' Carl said hurriedly. 'We'll just keep our fingers crossed.'

Adam nodded and broke into a run, heading for home.

'Oh, and Adam, if you don't get a Porsche, don't forget those German cars,' Jason yelled after him.

Adam slowed, puzzled, his excuse for getting away already forgotten. 'What?'

'You know, that car you're buying. Volkswagens. Passat, I think it's called. Passes everything in front of it, my dad says.'

'Right,' Adam waved. And accelerated rapidly.

Two

The rain was pelting down as the luxury coach swung between the wrought-iron gates of what one newspaper writer had described as 'the most aristocratic training ground possessed by any League football club'. Surrounded on three sides by oak and beech and ash, it was indeed a choice setting and the players themselves sometimes tended to boast about it. They liked its seclusion as well as the quality of the turf; but on a morning like this they preferred to remain in the coach and play cards or sit in the changing-room and gossip. Hardly any of them enjoyed playing in the rain, let alone training in the stuff.

Rob Heanor, however, had other ideas. In his view, professional footballers weren't just paid to play in front of the general public; they were paid to train, to get fit, to improve their skills and to listen to him. They were paid to train at certain times each week and when that time came it didn't matter one iota to Rob whether the sun was shining or snow was falling. They would train.

When the bus slid to a stop in front of the pavilion-like building, everyone knew that in a few minutes they'd all be going through the Tuesday morning torture chamber, as Ricky Gannon called it. Adam didn't have any strong feelings about wet weather. True, it made the ball harder to handle and he had to wear gloves whereas he preferred to keep with bare hands. There was a greater risk of slipping on a greasy surface in the goalmouth and an attacker was more likely to put the boot in simply because he wasn't able to control his momentum, so he was in danger of getting a knock. The one advantage of rain was that it softened his landing area; when he dived or fell on a shoulder or elbow he was less likely to jar himself.

Adam's main concern, as usual, was to acquit himself well in training so that he wouldn't lose his place for the next match. It was only three weeks ago that he'd made his debut in a League match and, of course, there was no guarantee that he would continue to be first choice. He'd replaced the club's long-serving goal-keeper, Jake Keedwell, and Jake was determined to evict him. They hadn't really been rivals – at least, not as far as Adam was concerned. Adam had come up through the junior ranks to be Reserve team goal-keeper and he'd had only one season's experience at that level. There really wasn't any thought in his mind that he would get what he regarded as the ultimate promotion when the Boss called him into the office to say he was going to play him against Everton. His form, he knew, had been outstanding for several matches and his confidence was even higher. All the same, Jake was so well established that it seemed only an earthquake could dislodge him. His reliability was such that some newspapers were inclined to print his name as Keepwell – and it was no printing error!

Then, surprisingly, Jake had a couple of disastrous matches. Four of the five goals City conceded were attributed directly to such fundamental mistakes as missing his punch in a crowded goalmouth and dropping the ball when challenged. Apparently Jake was unable to explain his loss of form and the Boss really had no alternative but to replace him with the eager and promising Reserves keeper. Adam hadn't let Ian Fenn down. The fans and the local Press immediately hailed him as a new star.

Even so, every time the players trained together, Adam experienced worries about his own prospects. Would the coach or the Boss have a sudden change of heart and restore Jake Keedwell to his old position? Would Adam himself commit some monumental blunder that would prove he wasn't really fit to be trusted in City's goal? Would he fail some test of skill or character devised by the cunning Rob Heanor? Adam had to admit that Heanor tended to treat all players alike and didn't display any favouritism. Well, certainly not openly. He had no idea whether the coach liked him as a person better than the rather dour, un-demonstrative Jake. When Rob had something to say in praise of a player's performance he said it immediately and warmly, which, according to Ricky Gannon, a central defender who had been the rounds of several League clubs over the years, was rare. Most coaches, in his experience, simply blasted their players all the time however well they played during a session. The theory being that if you praised someone he promptly relaxed, thinking he'd done enough. Rob, on the other hand, worked on the principle that occasional well-aimed praise acted as a stimulus on the player con-cerned. Some of the more exuberant members of City's first-team squad had been known to react quite ecstati-cally when singled out by Heanor for special commen-dation.

Now, on this wretched morning with the downpour showing no signs of abating, the coach wasted not a moment in getting his players out on to the pitch. There was a volley of grumbles from some of the older ones when Heanor told them to hurry up if they wanted to avoid fines for lateness.

'You know the rules,' he told them forcefully. 'You've all signed contracts, so don't blame me. The sooner we all get out there and perform, the sooner we'll all be back in the warm and dry.'

He paused and then added with a significant lowering of his voice: 'Anyway, you'd better get yourselves in fighting trim because the Boss is coming down to join us. For all I know, he's got some team changes in mind. That, or a new strategy for the match with Villa.'

Adam lifted his face to the skies and let the rain wash over him as he trotted towards the centre of the pitch where the coach would put them into small groups for the first of the morning's warming-up exercises. Jake was looking thunderous and Adam hoped he wasn't going to be paired off with him. Usually the goalkeepers underwent some specialist training later on in the proceedings and then, of course, they couldn't avoid each other. First, though, everyone had to join in the general fitness games, as Rob described them.

'OK, Jake, Ricky, Adam, sprinting on to a goal kick. Over there,' Rob directed. 'And don't hang about. I want to see all three of you *working*, running like mad.'

Adam was aware that Jake had shot him a hard glance but was determined not to worry about Jake's attitude. As he was the current first-team keeper it was his right to go into goal first while the other two became outfield players with the task of outwitting each other and then trying to put the ball past him into the net. For all he knew, it could well be a ploy on the coach's part to have the two keepers competing directly with each other.

It was an extremely simple exercise and so its effectiveness depended entirely on the speed and determination of the players tackling it. With the others standing on either side of him on the goal-line, Adam took a goal-kick, sending the ball as far down the pitch as possible. In the instant that he kicked the ball the other two would race after it; whoever gained possession first, tried to keep control of the ball and then shoot it past the keeper into the net. If they scored a goal then they took the goalie's place for the next kick.

'Give it everything you've got, Adam,' Ricky recommended; and that was just what Adam intended. Ricky was one of your old-fashioned, tough-as-old-boots central defenders who moaned about most things that involved any real effort; at least, he did when management was present. But he never shirked when it came to the point: certainly he trained at least as hard as anyone else. Ricky didn't like to be defeated and that made him an invaluable member of the City team.

It was an enormous kick, one of the longest Adam had ever achieved: and all the more surprising because it was off a wet surface. As if he were about to win a gold medal on the athletics field, Ricky Gannon charged after the ball. Adam had expected that, but not that Jake would show just as much determination; if anything, the goalkeeper was the quicker off the mark. But then, that was one of his skills. Keedwell hadn't kept his place in City's side all these years without deserving it. His instinctive reactions to any situation in the penalty area were lightning fast: something that Adam tried to copy. Soon, though, Jake was slowing down and it was inevitable that Ricky would reach the ball first. Once he had it under control he ran straight at Jake, dummied to go past him one way and then went the other. Adam could see that Jake wanted to dive for the ball with his hands: but that wasn't allowed in this exercise. Whoever played out of goal was an outfield player for the duration of the session.

Jake tried a double-footed tackle which Ricky easily evaded. But Ricky paused to wave a warning finger at Jake, indicating that he should not employ dubious tactics again. Ricky was like that. He might try the occasional illegal trick himself but if any opponent committed a sin Ricky made sure everyone was aware of it. Then Ricky sprinted away towards goal with Jake toiling behind him.

Adam advanced to narrow the angle for the shot. The rain was now driving into his eyes giving Ricky another advantage. He had started to slow up and was trying to pick his spot. Switching his attention momentarily from the ball to the man, Adam saw that City's centre-back was eyeing up the top right-hand corner of the net. It was an obvious target for a natural right-footer. Suddenly he swung his boot, shooting a fraction sooner than Adam expected. Nonetheless, the shot didn't take him by surprise. He was already moving to his right on the tips of his toes, ready to leap to catch the ball. And catch it he did, quite comfortably just above head height.

'You were lucky there!' Ricky panted. He really had expected to score. Moreover, he rather fancied his own chances of keeping goal in a match, confident he wouldn't let City down. So, for more than one reason, it would have suited him to put the ball past young Skipsea.

'I'm too good for you, Ricky. You'll have to hit 'em harder than that,' Adam taunted him. Three weeks ago he would never have dared talk to a senior player like that. But now he believed he was deservedly a member of the same team; and real team-mates respected, and joked with, one another.

They had to wait a few minutes for Jake, who hadn't said a word to either of them, to line up for the next goal-kick.

Further down the pitch, other trios were hard at work and Rob was going the rounds to see that no one was slacking. It looked as though he might be heading in their direction next. Adam noticed that Jake was keeping an eye on the coach and he could guess why. He was probably waiting for the manager to appear so that he could impress him with his endeavour as well as his skill.

Ricky was rather slower off the mark when Adam kicked the ball out again, whereas Jake went after it like a greyhound out of a trap. Adam guessed that this time Ricky was playing a different game; no doubt he was certain he could win the ball off his opponent without too much trouble. That was very much the centre-back's approach to a League match. Just occasionally, such confidence was misplaced and the rest of the defence suffered the consequences.

Jake, like most goalkeepers, enjoyed being an outfield player when the chance arose and he was by no means the worst footballer at the club. Now, trapping the ball cleanly, he pulled it round with the sole of his boot and then began to approach the goal, taptapping along in a come-and-take-it-off-me fashion. Ricky wasn't going to rise to the bait and make a tackle until he judged the moment to be absolutely right. Adam was enjoying the confrontation. The more these two players took out of themselves the less likely they were to beat him with the final shot. Or so he thought.

Ricky retreated centimetre by centimetre, though never for an instant taking his eyes off his opponent.

'Come on, then, Gannon, what're you waiting for?' Jake demanded, plainly annoyed at not being challenged. Ricky merely turned on a wolfish grin without answering. Jake decided to accelerate and, just as he did so, Ricky pounced. For once, however, his tackle was mistimed. His right foot simply scraped along the sodden turf, missing the ball and his opponent's instep by quite a margin.

With a yell of pleasure Jake surged forward and Ricky had to turn, fast, and give chase. Because he wasn't used to being a real goal-scorer, Jake slowed up fractionally before deciding where to place his shot. Adam had advanced to throw him off his stride, but it was Ricky's recovery rather than Adam's presence that prevented Jake from achieving his objective. Just as he was drawing back his right foot to shoot, Ricky reached him and managed to clip his heel. Jake was thrown off-balance and tumbled; yet somehow he still managed to strike the ball which, cannoning off Ricky's knee, flew in an arc over Adam's head and towards the roof of the net.

Adam turned instantly, making a frenzied effort to keep it out of his goal. With a huge leap he just managed to reach it and, with the back of his fingers, tried to deflect it over the bar. He almost succeeded. But then it struck the underside of the crossbar and ricocheted into the net after bouncing once on the goal-line. To Adam's great astonishment, both players instantly claimed they'd scored.

'Course it was mine!' Jake yelled with a fierceness Adam hadn't heard from him for a long time. 'I was shooting when you fouled me, Gannon! The ball was always going right into the back of the net.'

'Nuts!' Ricky replied tersely. 'You made a hash of hitting it and the ball came off my leg. So it counts as an own-goal, scored by me! You saw that, didn't you, Adam?'

Adam shook his head decisively. He wasn't going to get into an argument. 'Couldn't tell,' he said. 'All I know is it was a fluke and –'

'Rubbish!' Jake shouted and Adam knew he'd said the wrong thing. 'It's not a fluke if you succeed in what you're trying to do. I've heard that often enough from strikers trying to beat *me*!'

'Look, I said I couldn't be sure, Jake. All I was thinking about was keeping the ball out of the net. Almost managed it, too.'

'But you *didn't*, son. That's the point,' Ricky exclaimed. 'And the ball definitely went off me. So I should go in goal.'

'You can't have an advantage for yourself off an own-goal! That's preposterous,' Jake stormed back. 'Let's get this straight, Adam. How about some support from a fellow goalie?'

'You can't be serious, Jake!' Ricky interrupted. 'How can you expect Adam to be on your side when you're deadly rivals?'

For a moment there was complete silence.

'That, er, doesn't come into it, Ricky,' Adam said. He felt embarrassed and he suspected he looked it. He was anxious not to catch Jake's eye, but his mistake was not to deny at once that he and Jake were rivals. 'I can't give a real opinion. Like I said, I didn't see who touched the ball last. Anyway, what does it matter? I don't care who goes in goal next. I missed it, so I play out.'

'If we're doing this thing for real then we stick to the rules,' Jake said heatedly. 'I scored the goal and –'

'No way!' Ricky retaliated with equal force.

Suddenly, Rob Heanor was in their midst. To their

surprise, he beamed at them. 'Good to hear you take everything so keenly you fall out over a goal. Great. What's the argument about?'

Adam supposed that the others, too, would realise how trivial the entire dispute was and say it wasn't worth talking about. He was quite wrong.

'I scored a goal and Gannon here claimed the ball came off him,' Jake explained unrelentingly. 'Young Adam says he didn't see who touched the ball last. But he couldn't keep it out of the net.'

Ricky actually snorted. 'Nuts! I intercepted it and the ball went in off me. I'll tell you something that'll make you laugh, Rob. Jake says if it did go in off me it was an own-goal and I shouldn't get the credit! He's going round the twist.'

Rob shot a quick glance at the senior goalkeeper to see how he was taking the insult, but he didn't reprove Ricky. Perhaps, thought Adam, the coach had the same opinion. If he did, then that buttressed his own position in the first-team squad.

'Well, there's an easy way of settling this,' Heanor announced with another smile. 'Toss up and the winner goes in goal. Seems fairest to me.'

From a pocket he produced a coin and with the flourish of a conjuror announced, 'Heads Jake, tails Ricky.' He sent the coin spinning high in the air. Inevitably, he also made a production number out of catching it, slapping it on his wrist and then revealing the outcome.

'You win, Jake, so you go into goal.'

In fact, nobody had been near enough to Rob to see which way the coin had landed. Adam sensed that Rob had already made up his mind what the outcome would be. The coach wasn't the sort of guy who'd leave anything to chance if he could help it. Anyway, it was certainly the wisest decision because Jake was so eager to be the winner. Ricky now looked as if he didn't know what all the fuss had been about in the first place.

Clearly delighted to be between the posts again, Jake delivered one of his most powerful kicks (and, in his heyday, he'd been renowned for the length of his dead-ball kicking) but then slithered on the rain-slicked turf. He didn't lose his balance but he was annoyed with himself. Heanor, he was sure, would have taken note of that slip. The ball, meanwhile, was in Adam's possession. Once again, Ricky hadn't bothered to put much effort into the chase; he was content to back himself to win the ball in a tackle whoever he faced.

However, Adam had worked out a different ploy from Jake's. Instead of taking the ball right up to his opponent he suddenly lifted it hard and high over Ricky's head and immediately sprinted after it. Taken by surprise, Ricky hesitated and lost valuable time looking up at the ball when he should have chased it. Adam, who'd always been quick off the mark and prac- tised his sprints from blocks daily, easily regained pos- session. His only concern now was how to beat the goalkeeper. Jake, naturally, hadn't taken his eyes off the ball and began a positive advance to narrow the angle for Adam's shot.

But the goalkeeper was taken by surprise too because Adam fired in a shot which Jake had not antici- pated. An experienced forward would have waited until he was at least a couple of strides nearer goal. Adam, though, not only hit the ball hard and from further away, but his aim was perfect. The ball flew arrow-like over Jake's shoulder and lifted the net off its moorings.

'Great shot, son!' Rob Heanor exclaimed, and meant it.

Adam was so elated he felt like turning a cartwheel. Although he'd scored often in junior football, and even shone when tried out on the wing in City's third team during an injury crisis, no goal had been as good as this one. Not even Ian Fenn, famed for his spectacular goals, could have improved on that shot.

Jake was still shaking his head in bewilderment as Rob Heanor came across to pat Adam on the back and then usher him towards the net.

'If you can score like that I don't know what the hell I'm doing keeping you in goal,' he said. 'I just wish a few of our strikers had that sort of eye for goal. Anyway, son, get yourself set up to stop a few before we get on to the next exercise. The Boss'll be down in a minute. Wish he'd arrived in time to see that cracker.'

Neither Jake nor Ricky seemed inclined to try very hard to defeat one another in the remaining minutes devoted to the first exercise. It was as if they knew everything was going Adam's way and there was no point in risking their tempers or using up energy to take his place in goal. So Adam was reduced to the role of spectator as his rivals simply played with the ball on the edge of the penalty area.

Then Ian Fenn arrived and players' attitudes instantly changed.

Three

As a schoolboy, Adam had been one of Ian Fenn's
greatest admirers. In those days, Ian played for Spurs
and would probably have gained a trunkful of England
caps if only he'd been a few centimetres taller and
hadn't had to face such fierce competition as both a
goal-scorer and playmaker. Paradoxically, it was his
very versatility that counted against him. The England
manager at that time preferred players who were the
best of their kind at *one* particular skill. Despite this,
Ian had got into the England squad and even on to
the pitch for one game against Finland; and in that
one match his misfortune was to suffer an ankle injury
just after half-time. The player who substituted for
him turned on a brilliant display as a creative midfielder and became a fixture in the team. So, when
his ankle healed, Ian Fenn couldn't get back into the
side. It was the sort of fate that had befallen plenty
of talented professionals over the years but, unlike
others, Ian Fenn didn't just moan about it. He looked
to the future, not the past; which, of course, was just
how it had to be for a football manager.

The season following his England debut, Ian suffered
another setback. Spurs signed a Paraguayan international who, though hardly a centimetre taller than

Fenn, slotted into the team as if he'd been in touch with everyone for years. As if to emphasize his stature, he also scored a hat-trick in his first match and thereafter could hardly put a foot wrong as far as supporters and management were concerned. Ian lost out again; and Reserve-team football held little attraction for him. One or two clubs in lower divisions, as well as one Midland club in the First, made inquiries about him, but either the terms were unappealing or Ian simply didn't fancy the club's prospects.

Just as he was resigning himself either to a long spell in the Reserves or a move out of football altogether, the offer came from City to be their player-manager. City had been hovering on the fringes of promotion from the Second Division for several seasons. But no one had been able to provide the push that would get them into the promised land. Their Chairman believed what they needed was a young man with charisma, flair, experience and ambition, who could also provide true leadership on the pitch itself. He decided, on the evidence of his own eyes as a spectator and on what he learned from fellow football directors, that Ian Fenn as the man he wanted.

Ian hadn't let him down. In his first full season he'd taken the team up into the First Division. He said at the time that the squad wasn't strong enough to make much impact in the top flight but, as it turned out, City had survived comfortably enough and with only a small amount of money being spent on reinforcements. Now, in the early stages of a new season, Ian's third in charge of the club, City's supporters were hoping for real success. They recognised that the Championship was probably beyond them, but victory in one of the Cup competitions was what everyone had set their hearts on. Including, naturally enough, the young Manager himself.

Now he watched intently as Rob Heanor switched the squad from one exercise to another. This one was designed to improve passing while warming up for the remainder of the session and most coaches who favoured it would have used it ahead of the 'chasing-a-goal-kick' game. But Heanor liked to be different at all times, and especially when the Boss was around. He'd been at the club when Ian arrived and, Adam supposed, must have felt that his job was at risk. Most new managers preferred to bring their own coaching staff with them, or at least recruit them personally from elsewhere.

Ian, however, seemed perfectly content with Heanor's style and abilities and he scarcely ever recommended changes to the coach's programme. Ian himself was still playing regularly and from time to time joined in training sessions, accepting Rob's instructions without demur, just like any other player. But he wasn't participating in the 'all-change-in-the-circle' exercise. The 16-strong squad was split with each set of eight forming a circle. Once the ball was on the move a player could pass to anyone he liked and then, as he did so, had to dash across to take the place of the player who'd received the pass; and the receiver sent the ball on to someone else and took *his* place; and so it continued until the coach deemed it time to switch to something else.

When the stint was over and the players were given a five-minute break, Rob Heanor took Adam on one side. 'I can see you're in good form, son,' he said with an approving smile. 'Getting into the first team's given your confidence a big boost and that shows. But don't start to think that everything's perfect. We've still got things to work on with your keeping. Agreed?'

Adam was in no position to argue though he had no idea what the coach was getting at, but it was part of Heanor's style to get players to analyse their own strengths and weaknesses. Few of them, however, were good at that; they weren't even capable of assessing other players' qualities off and on the pitch.

'Er, sure, Coach,' Adam muttered.

'So what do you reckon you need to improve?'

Adam couldn't imagine what he ought to say. There were so many aspects of a goalkeeper's role that could be improved in his case, or indeed in anyone's case. After all, he supposed that even the current England goalkeeper would admit *his* keeping wasn't perfect.

'Er, my timing?' he suggested.

'Always room for improvement in that department, son. For *everyone*. Timing's instinct, really, and you either have it or you don't. Your instinct's pretty good, otherwise you wouldn't be in the first team at this club. But even when you have it, sometimes it lets you down. So, be a bit more specific than that. Try again.'

Rapidly Adam ran through a few possibilities in his mind: kicking, distribution, positioning at corners and free kicks on the edge of the box, jumping for crosses. Then he recalled an error he'd committed against Everton. 'My punching?' he said, only a little tentatively.

'Well done! I knew you were a smart lad, Adam. Yeah, it's something that we've definitely got to work on. Punching's very important in the right situation, in a goalmouth crowded with big fellers. So you've got to reach the ball with your fist and make sure you punch it well clear. What happened against Everton?'

'I missed the ball altogether. Well, almost . . .'

'You're right. You *missed*. Lucky for us Ricky Gannon was around to pick up the pieces and get the ball away. Otherwise we could have been in big trouble.

That nippy little striker Everton have wouldn't have made any mistake if he'd been in range at that moment. So what should you have done. ?'

Adam was surprised. He'd just explained that he knew what had gone wrong and therefore he also knew how to rectify it. 'Make sure I get to the ball with my fist ready? I mean, what . . .'

He really didn't know what else he could say. But, clearly, Rob Heanor had something else in mind. The coach waited a few moments while his young goal-keeper pondered the problem and then decided to provide a clue.

'Which hand did you use?'

'The right, of course. I mean –'

'There's no of course about it, son! You have to use the hand that's best placed for dealing with the problem. Against Everton your mistake was not just to miss the ball with your right hand. It was that you used the wrong hand. What was wrong with your left fist?'

'Er, nothing, really. Except that it's not as strong as my right. I'm not so confident about using it.'

'Exactly! And that's what we've got to work on, young Adam. A goalkeeper's got to be capable of using both hands equally well. It's called being ambidextrous, if you didn't know.'

Rob Heanor treated himself to a broad smile for getting both the word and the explanation out. Now and again, he, like most players and ex-players, couldn't resist showing off something in his repertoire. Adam did know the word but he didn't think he'd ever used it. There was nothing to be gained, though, by trying to look smart so he just nodded as if he'd learned something from his mentor.

'So, we're going to get you working hard on the old

punchbag,' the coach resumed. 'Hitting hard, hitting left, right, *left*. Fix a rhythm. Get the elbows going, elbows are very important for a goalkeeper. Rhythm: that's vital. Get you to the stage where it seems as natural to use the left as the right. So you don't at any point think which hand you're going to use. You use whichever is right – correction! – the most effective. Got it?'

Adam nodded positively. He was thinking about Rob's automatic correction. Was it a deliberate mistake or not? It was the sort of trick the coach would enjoy pulling off. Anyway, it had worked. Adam got the message.

'OK, so that's one point we've got over. Now, does that give you any clues to the next one?'

This was beginning to seem like the worst kind of interrogation ever. Adam wondered if the coach was putting him through it just to cut him down to size or whether he really did believe he had so much to learn. He'd been told many times, and he knew it, that above all else a goalie has to possess confidence. Without it, he might as well give up and become a refuse collector or something else that didn't make any demands on your temperament. Yet Rob Heanor now seemed determined to undermine Adam's faith in himself. He could see that the coach wasn't going to help him out with any of his own clues so he shook his head.

'Well, it should, so come on, Adam, you've got to do some work here. Can't leave it all to me. My job is to bring out the best in you. I can't do that if you won't cooperate. Think back, what hand were we talking about?'

'The left.' Resignedly now.

'Exactly! So we have to start improving on that side so that everything matches up. You've got to be just as good *jumping* to the left, *diving* to the left, *falling* to the left. And, at this minute in time, you're not. You're better on the right. Think about it a moment and you'll agree, I'm sure.'

Before Adam could respond, Heanor turned and walked away to talk to the rest of the squad, leaving Adam to do precisely what he'd been told. It was another of the coach's tactical moves in his relationship with players under his command. Adam, however, didn't need to be won over: he was perfectly willing to admit he still had a lot to learn. He was prepared to follow whatever course of action the coach insisted on. But he did wish Rob Heanor wouldn't treat him, and other players, like a child – and a naughty child at that.

Having issued further instructions and left the rest of the squad in the charge of Alex Hart, the physio, Heanor returned to his young goalkeeper. He didn't ask any more questions. The time for words was over.

'Come here, son,' he beckoned after picking up a spare ball. 'Let's give The Wall some hammer.'

Four

The Wall loomed large in everyone's mind – it could be a torture zone for any player. But the club's goal-keepers viewed it with probably the greatest foreboding. It was where their reflexes could be tested as nowhere else. The wall really wasn't very high – hardly more than six feet – but, in a psychological sense, it was a mountain. Adam, who'd already had some bad moments there in the past year, followed Heanor with a lurching stomach and a sinking heart.

'Right, Goalie, stand just here – and be ready for anything,' the coach ordered, pointing to a spot between three and four metres from the brick-and-wood structure (it contained different materials in order to provide a variety of surfaces for the ball to rebound from). 'Just make sure you don't miss a thing.'

The 'game', as Rob (but none of the team) thought of it, was simple enough; but it was also physically exhausting and nerve-wracking. Standing just behind the player involved, but completely out of his line of vision, the coach would kick or hurl the ball against the wall from whatever angle he chose: and the player had to catch it on the rebound, before it reached the ground. Then, without delay, the player had to return the ball to the coach for the next 'catch'. Just how long the exercise lasted depended entirely on the whim of the coach.

Adam knew that it was his left-side reflexes that were to be tested but, as he'd supposed, Rob started the game with a volley to the right. The first shot was quite soft and that meant he had to dive full-length to catch the gentle rebound. With the rain still bucketing down the ground was becoming quite slippery, but at least it wasn't jarring.

Rather fortuitously, Adam managed to grab the ball just before it touched the turf and then, in approved fashion, cradled it in the pit of his stomach before tossing it to Rob: who, predictably, didn't say a word about the quality of the catch or make any comment at all. The coach was thinking only about where to aim the next shot. The sequence was predictably unpredictable: first, four shots to the right, then one left, another that might have been intended for the left but was actually central and then back to the right again. It was only when Adam missed a comparatively easy catch to the right that Heanor spoke. Surprisingly, his words were mild: 'You shouldn't have slipped up there, son. That was a gift. Concentrate.'

Concentration was a major topic of Rob's, especially when talking to his goalkeeper. And, of course, it couldn't be denied that it wasn't hard for a keeper to switch off when his team was attacking incessantly and there was no sign of the opposition being capable of managing a break-out from defence. Forty-five minutes was a long, long time in which to think about nothing but how to deal with the next shot that might come your way. The second spell of forty-five minutes might be harder still if the match had declined into a tedious midfield muddle. So every goalie suffered lapses of concentration during the course of a game.

31

The trick was to conceal them from the opposition and your own manager and coach. Rob, being Rob, didn't relent if he spotted what he considered a relaxed moment in his goalkeeper's life. He hammered away at this lack of diligence as if it were the greatest sin in the world. Perhaps, in his eyes, it was. But Adam only had to hear the word 'concentration' used in normal conversation or in a broadcast about some quite ordinary aspect of life and instantaneously an image of Rob Heanor in lecturing pose flashed into his mind. Adam supposed that Jake Keedwell must react in much the same way.

Just when Adam was on the point of pleading for a break, Rob announced: 'OK, last shot coming up. Make sure you don't miss it.'

This time Adam guessed right – and the ball crashed against the left-hand side of the wall, rebounding at a steep angle from its contact with a slightly protruding brick. Hurling himself sideways he just succeeded in scooping it up before it could touch the grass. It was, he reckoned, his best 'save' of the entire morning in spite of his earlier feeling of exhaustion. To his relief, the coach shared his view.

'Well done, son, that was a good 'un. You've kept going well because I was really testing you out there. But don't relax yet! There's another game coming up. But you can have a one-minute break. OK?'

Adam groaned, audibly. But Rob Heanor didn't complain. If he'd been giving his players a tough time he expected them to protest. After all, their muscles and joints would be aching if they'd been tested properly. Rob's disapproval was voiced only when a player said he'd had enough.

Because he'd spent so much time on the ground, Adam wandered across to lean against The Wall for the duration of the break. Rob returned briskly to the main squad to see what they were achieving under Alex Hart's direction. Adam's thoughts almost automatically switched to food. Training sessions of this intensive nature could make him absolutely ravenous. That was partly due, he knew, to the fact that on training mornings he didn't eat much breakfast, not wanting to risk losing it because of the rigorous routines. It was much safer to have a meal when training was over for the day. Perhaps, tonight, he'd treat himself to a giant pizza with lots of side dishes and then chocolate ice-cream with –

'Thinking of your stomach, then? How best you can fill it?'

Rob Heanor's questions drilled right through him and he felt himself colouring up.

'No, no, not really,' Adam denied instantly, wondering how he could have missed seeing the coach return. His eyes had closed for only a second.

'Come off it! You can't kid me. They used to say that armies marched on their stomachs. Well, I could tell 'em footballers are just the same, always thinking of what they can stuff themselves with when the training staff aren't around.'

'Well, I was thinking about going out for a meal tonight,' Adam admitted cautiously.

'I'd forget about that, son. Boss has got a little job for you tonight that'll keep you out of mischief. No, don't ask me about it. He'll tell you himself. Our job now is to get back to work. Got to get you toned up properly.'

The next exercise was the toughest of the lot, in Adam's experience. The first time he'd been subjected to it he was literally sick afterwards. His stomach muscles felt as if they'd been trampled on by a herd of elephants. Hours later he was still in pain and would have thrown up again if there'd been anything inside him to eject. First, he had to sit on the ground and reach, or jump up, to catch a ball thrown above the level of his head; and, if he succeeded, he then had to stand up to throw the ball back to the coach before returning to sitting position for the next throw. When that exercise was kept up continuously for only half-a-minute the catcher was exhausted and almost ready to commit suicide to get out of reaching for the next ball. Rob didn't relent for what seemed like eternity, but was only just over a minute.

'OK, you did well there, son,' the coach praised him as he allowed Adam to take a breather. Adam barely heard the words. Hands on hips, trunk leaning forward, he was gasping for air. His limbs felt as if they'd been flayed with strings of lead weights. There was pain everywhere.

Rob Heaner, though, still wasn't satisfied. Adam knew the worst part was still to come. The goalkeeper had to lie flat on his already ravaged stomach and then raise his body, without using his hands, of course, to catch a ball thrown at him from a variety of distances. The idea was to simulate match conditions and a situation where the goalkeeper had made a save, been unable to hold on to the ball and was forced, while lying prone, to make an effort to grab it during a typical goalmouth scramble.

Adam wanted to appeal for mercy. He'd done enough to show that he was both competent and fit. Even if there was a weakness on his left side, this latest sequence in the torture chamber was hardly likely to correct it. When you were rising from the prone position there wasn't much chance of being able to twist to one side as well and still hope to catch the ball!

Heanor, however, made sure that Adam did some work on his weaker side by telling him to parry the ball if he couldn't catch it – and then hurling it towards him as hard as he could. Invariably now, he threw to Adam's left. The goalkeeper managed to catch and then deflect the ball at least a dozen times before he simply was unable to take the pace. His stomach, back and shoulder muscles couldn't cope with these exertions any longer. Adam collapsed, face down, and nothing on earth could have made him get to his feet at that moment.

And Rob Heanor recognised that.

'OK, son, take your time,' he advised, in avuncular fashion. 'You've worked well and deserve a rest. D'you think things got a bit better there on the left side?'

Adam still hadn't enough strength to speak properly so he nodded, feebly. That was enough for the coach. For once, Heanor wondered if he'd gone just a little too far. The lad certainly looked shattered. But young bodies recovered quickly. That was one of the benefits of Ian Fenn's regime. If your squad mostly consisted of youngsters then you didn't have to worry so much about ankles and knees and tendons and all the football strains imaginable. You weren't always trying to find replacements for older players who had dropped out of training because of a nagging injury or rapidly-advancing senility. Young players could take plenty of hammer and still come back for more, just as long as you kept offering them the right sort of incentives: like a place in the first-team squad.

'Come on then, son, let's have you on your feet.' Heanor couldn't bring himself to offer a helping hand and Adam certainly wouldn't have expected it. 'No good comes of lying on wet grass too long, you know.'

With a groan that he made no effort to repress, Adam

rolled on his back, took a couple of deep breaths, and then forced himself to stand up. He thought he'd detected a worried note in the coach's voice. But he couldn't work out whether Rob was worried about his stamina or the severity of the punishment inflicted on him. In one way, Adam was elated: he'd been driven through a pain barrier and survived it. This time he hadn't been physically sick, although he sensed he was close to it a couple of minutes before the coach called a halt.

Rob was relieved to see his young goalkeeper on his feet and, now that he was, he put an arm round his shoulders, a rare gesture.

'That's it, then, Adam. But before you have your bath, go and see the Boss. He's back in his office now.' The coach paused, finding the right words for his final message. 'Keep thinking about that weakness on the left. Anything you can do to improve in that direction'll get my support. Tomorrow we'll have a good go on the punchbag. OK?'

Adam nodded again. He wondered why the manager wanted to see him. Surely he hadn't done anything wrong? His stomach began to churn as he knocked at the door of the tiny office opposite the changing-rooms.

'Things go well this morning, Adam?'

'Yeah, fine, Boss.' Adam suspected that his exhaustion must show on his face, but he would never admit to it.

The Manager nodded. 'Good. The sort of training you were doing this morning is vital. So it shouldn't be interrupted by personal phone calls, you know. Understand?'

Adam was totally baffled. 'No, Boss, I don't. Haven't a clue.'

Fenn shrugged. 'Well, some guy telephoned here, wanting a word with you. I thought he must know you, that you'd told him he could contact you at the training ground.'

'No, Boss, definitely not! I'd never do that.' Adam was adamant. He couldn't imagine who his caller might be. His mates certainly wouldn't ring him at the football club, let alone at the training ground. It was a complete mystery.

'Oh, well, could've been some journalist trying a sneaky approach for an interview, I suppose. Still, if you didn't authorise it, no blame attaches to you.' He paused momentarily and then went on: 'Look, something I want you to do for us – for the Club – tonight. Present the prizes at an indoor six-a-side tournament out at Tanton – you know, that villagey place on the other side of the moor. It's nice for them to have a professional player to hand over the Cup and the medals and you know the Club's always keen on publicity where youngsters are involved. So, bit of prestige and goodwill all round. You can manage that, can't you?'

Ian Fenn had always possessed a winning smile and now he positively beamed at Adam. It wasn't strictly necessary because no newcomer to City's first-team squad would dare refuse such an undemanding request from the manager. But Ian's regard for his teenage goalkeeper was higher than Adam ever imagined.

'Oh, sure, Boss. What –'

'Fine, fine,' the manager cut in briskly. 'I'm sure they'll look after you all right. Just ask for Bob Boscombe when you get there and he'll tell you what's wanted. Starts at the Leisure Centre at seven-thirty but I reckon you could turn up a bit after that if you wanted to. The *Evening Mail* will be sending a photographer so get yourself pictured with the winners. Fair enough? Good. Right, you've had one soaking this morning. Now go and have another – a hot one this time!'

Ian Fenn rarely joined his players in the colossal communal bath, perhaps to underline the point that fraternization could go too far. After all, it wasn't easy to share a bath with a bloke you were about to fine one hundred pounds for an act of ill-discipline or bawl out for a bad performance on the pitch. Bosses had to stay aloof at times.

The only other player who tended to keep apart at bath time was Jake Keedwell, so Adam wasn't able to discover what mood his so-called rival was in now that training was over for the day. The rest of the squad, however, were in excellent spirits and full of a party most of them were going to that night. Adam felt a tinge of disappointment that he hadn't been invited.

As if sensing that Adam might feel excluded, Karl Holliday grinned at him and inquired: 'Got a date tonight, then Skips?'

Adam grimaced. 'Not exactly. Got to go and present some prizes for the Boss at a six-a-side tournament.'

Ricky Gannon laughed. 'Oh, you got landed with that one, did you, Adam? I reckon the Boss must've been thinking he'd have to do the job himself when he heard how many of the lads were off to Nigel's party. You must've saved the day – well, the night for him. Hey, that's not bad, is it? Adam the goalie saved the Boss...'

Nobody else appeared to think it was hilarious, but Karl, a lively, electric winger who couldn't resist thinking up a nickname for every player he knew, gave Adam a sympathetic smile.

'Hard luck, mate. Where is it?'

'Tanton.'

'Oh, tough. Be a real drag going all that way just for a prize-giving. Still, it'll sure keep you out of mischief as long as you don't drink and drive!'

Until that moment, Adam hadn't given a thought to how he was going to get to and from Tanton Leisure Centre.

Five

In the kitchen, Adam sliced into a stoneground brown loaf, put the toaster on and opened a can of baked beans. He felt absolutely ravenous and the evening meal was too far away to contemplate waiting.

'What have you been doing today?' his mother asked, walking into the kitchen. 'You look terrible.'

'Thanks,' Adam replied laconically.

'No, seriously, Adam. You look drained. Worn out. And you normally don't eat at this time of day – well, not energy food, anyway.'

'I'm just hungry, that's all. We had an extra-tough training session this morning. The coach thinks we're not all as fit as we ought to be. So he turned on the pressure-tap. Nothing unusual in that.'

He busied himself with the pan of beans. His mother had been busy in the study, working on some sales figures and he'd hoped not to disturb her when he returned from the training ground. Inquisitions were always best avoided. Now she deftly removed two slices of slightly scorched toast from the badly-programmed toaster and started to butter them. 'Aren't those beans done?' she asked. And then added in the same tone: 'If training is going to wear you out like this you'd be better off with a different job. A job where your health isn't at stake.'

'Mum, there's nothing wrong with my job,' Adam replied, exasperated. 'The whole point of playing sport is to be fit, and professional sport makes sure you are fit. The coach knows what he's doing, he never pushes anyone too far. Wouldn't be much point in that, would there? I mean, if a player was too exhausted, too far gone, to play properly for the team then the Club would suffer. Rob Heanor is a fully-qualified coach, F.A. badges and all that, and –'

'Qualifications aren't everything, Adam. It's the man himself who matters. Some of these fitness maniacs just don't seem to understand how lesser mortals – less fit mortals, if you like – can suffer by being pushed too far. The victim doesn't complain and so the screws are kept on. That's when trouble starts. Look, I should know. I suffered under a crazy PE teacher at my school and I was too innocent to know I should have pulled out, so I used to end up in agony.'

'But it isn't like that at –'

'I vowed later it would never happen to my children, if I had any,' she continued as if he'd never spoken. 'If you're going to come home looking as shattered as you do now then it's time to take a new look at this job of yours. I mean it.'

Adam swallowed a mouthful of beans and toast and sighed deeply. 'Mum, forget it, will you? I just had an extra-tough session today. Rob thinks I could improve a bit in a couple of ways, that's all, so we worked a bit longer. And maybe I should have had a real breakfast. OK?'

His mother didn't dispute that. Sometimes she developed obsessions about her family or her own life-style and it was difficult to deflect her when she launched herself into her latest one. It was true that

41

he had felt shattered by the time he reached home but already the food was doing him good.

'D'you think Dad will be able to spare the car tonight?' he asked.

'Why, where do you want to go?'

Adam sighed again. Was there to be another drawn-out tennis match of questions and answers volleyed back and forth across the net of domestic debate? Why couldn't she just say 'yes' or 'no' or even 'maybe'?

'Tanton Leisure Centre. Got to present some prizes for an indoor tournament. The Boss asked me specially to do it.'

Mrs Skipsea raised an elegant eyebrow. 'So if you're doing it on behalf of the Club why aren't they providing you with transport?'

'Look, Mum, they don't have spare cars for every-body all the time! The regular players can afford their own. I'll be in the same position before long, the way things are going. But I haven't got there yet. Honestly, I'm sure Dad won't mind if the car is free. And, anyway, being asked to do this prize-giving is really a bit of an honour. He could've asked plenty of other people. So I can't go laying down conditions, can I?'

'Well, actually, your Dad did say he might be late tonight because he's got a meeting somewhere. So you're probably out of luck, anyway. You'll have to try elsewhere.'

Adam cursed inaudibly. Now he was down to one possibility, and that was more likely to be an improb-ability. 'What time is Zoe going to be home?' he asked.

'Late. And I hope you're not going to ask to borrow her car. That wouldn't be fair at all. You know how she saved like mad to buy that car. If anything hap-pened to it . . .'

'I wouldn't harm her car. I'm as good a driver as

42

anyone in this family!'

'That's your view. It's not Mrs Benson's. The last time she saw you driving Zoe's car she was shocked by the way you took the corner on Higher Lane on almost two wheels. So she said, anyway.'

'That's not true!' He was indignant. 'Mrs Benson is no judge of anything. Did she tell you that herself?'

'She did.'

'Well, if she told you, she'd tell Zoe as well. That's the sort of sneak she is. But Zoe's never said a word to me about it.'

'Look, Adam, I know your sister's always thought the sun shines out of your eyes, right from the time you were a baby. But she doesn't think you're perfect in every way. Zoe has a mind of her own even where you're concerned.'

Adam swallowed the last remnants of his snack and felt better. 'Is she working overtime again tonight?'

'These days I never know what any of you are up to. This house gets more like a motel by the minute.'

Adam got up and made a point of washing plates, mugs, saucepan and cutlery with comprehensive enthusiasm. With his mother in this uncooperative mood, he might as well retire to his room and enjoy his own company. So, when she disappeared into her study again, he crept upstairs, picked up a horror novel he'd started the previous night and switched on his favourite music at a reduced volume to avoid a peremptory call from downstairs.

But, after a few minutes, he jack-knifed off his bed and walked across to the window. He was unable to remain inactive with the problem of how to get to Tanton unresolved. Buses didn't run regularly on that route (well, not in the evening) and a taxi-ride would cost him a fortune; the Club might recompense him for that sort of expenditure but he couldn't bet on it. So what was he going to do?

Adam's room overlooked the Avenue and at that moment by sheer luck he caught sight of his mother crossing the road, clearly on her way to a social visit. So he had the house to himself for at least a few minutes. He dashed downstairs and into the study. The telephone number of the old people's home where his sister worked headed the list on the message-board in front of him, so he didn't need to waste time looking it up. Seabright Villas was a retirement complex with residential care and instant medical facilities and goodness knew what else to make the wealthy elderly happy in their final years. He dialled the number.

He was out of luck. Or was he? A voice at the other end told him that Miss Skipsea wasn't available; but that might mean she'd already left for home. Adam thought of asking for Mr Kelleher, her boss; she was close to him and he would probably know where she was. But Adam realised that it wouldn't be fair to turn his own worries into an emergency for Zoe by inventing an excuse for bothering Mark Kelleher. Reluctantly, he replaced the receiver and tried to work out what he must do if Zoe didn't return home soon and lend him her Fiat. The only worthwhile idea that crossed his mind was to hire a car but, not being familiar with the ways of the car-hire business, he suspected it was probably too late in the day for that.

Feeling annoyed with everyone for letting him down, Adam threw himself on to his bed – and then remembered that, with his mother out of the house, he could turn up his music. So he did, deafeningly for ten defiant minutes. He also tried to return to his book but he couldn't concentrate on what was becoming not so much a fantastic story, but a story that was too fantastic for such ordinary words. Disappointed again, he put the book down, lowered the music volume and laced his fingers behind his head.

Then, to his great relief, he heard a car pull into the drive. He knew from the sound of the engine that it was Zoe.

He ambushed her as she came up the stairs. His smile was at its widest, in contrast to her own frown and apparent weariness. But Adam didn't really notice. To him Zoe was always glamorous, the sort of sister other men immediately commented on and tried to date.

'Hi! Had a good day, sister Zoe?'

'Not particularly. And I do wish you'd stop calling me that. You don't have to keep reminding me that I work in a nursing home. And I'm not likely to forget I'm your sister, am I?'

It wasn't like her to object to one of his jokes, especially one as innocuous as that. Something had definitely gone wrong in her day. So, abashed, he asked what it was.

'Oh, all sorts, really. Things are just so hectic at the moment. Old folk are so demanding, so exhausting. As if you've nothing else to do but make life merry for them every spare minute of the day. Honestly, sometimes I could scream.'

For a moment she leaned against the bannisters and ran her fingers through her mane of shoulder-length, wavy, highlighted hair. Then, straightening up with a determined effort, she climbed the rest of the stairs and went into her bedroom to collapse on the bed.

Adam, anxious not to miss his opportunity, followed. Neither of them had made a thing out of keeping the other out of her or his room during their growing-up days.

'But I thought you loved the job,' he said, perching on her armchair, a family heirloom which Zoe regarded as her own. 'And you and Mark Kelleher get on'.

'Oh sure, like the proverbial house-fire. But, well, there are days when the old dears drive me up the wall. Anyway, I think I'm going to have a long, long bath and soak the stresses away.' She stood up. 'Is Mum out?'

'Yeah, she's visiting Mrs Thackray, I think. Deciding who to put up for election to their next committee, I expect.'

Zoe nodded. 'Good,' she said, taking off her jacket and then unzipping her skirt.

'Er, look, Zoe, are you going out tonight?' Adam inquired hastily.

She shook her head, stepping out of her skirt. 'No, I told you, I'm bushed. Got some medical stuff to read, anyway. Probably have an early night, too, because I know it's going to be a late one tomorrow. Mark's got a management meeting.'

'In that case, d'you think I could borrow the Fiat? I'll treat it like my own and –'

'Where're you going?'

'Out to Tanton. Ian Fenn's asked me to present the prizes at an indoor tournament.'

'Who with? Not some of your boozy team-mates? I'm not having my –'

'No, no, honestly! Going on my own. It's, you know, a bit of an honour, really, first time I've ever been asked to do something like this.'

Zoe paused. 'So you won't be giving anyone lifts or drinking or driving too fast to show off or anything like that?'

Adam made a great display of crossing his heart with both hands. 'Promise I won't. I'm really grateful,

Zoe, I wouldn't dream of doing a thing wrong. I know how much the car matters to you.'

'It's my independence, that's what it is. Well, go on, then, you can have it.' She started to unbutton her blouse. 'The keys are there in my bag. Just treat it like a car you had spent thousands on. OK?'

'Sure.' Deftly, he took the keys. 'Enjoy your bath. And thanks again, Zoe. You've definitely saved my life.'

Later he was to remember very clearly the strange look she gave him in answer to that casual remark.

It turned out to be a much more rewarding evening than he'd imagined. Just as the Boss had promised, Bob Boscombe, a bouncy, beaming character, welcomed him as if he were an England star doing them the greatest possible favour by making such a visit. Bob, who seemed to scuttle rather than walk, insisted on introducing him to just about every person who was present: and, indeed, it did appear that all of them wanted to shake his hand and compliment him on his performances for City.

No one remarked, as he'd feared they might, that it couldn't have been so long since he himself had played in a junior six-a-side tournament like this one. Even the players themselves gave the impression of being stunned by his presence, though they all eagerly addressed him as Adam and several half-shyly offered him autograph albums and programmes to sign. Of course, he'd been giving autographs for months, ever since he'd become the obvious understudy to Jake Keedwell. Yet it still gave him a thrill to be asked and he'd vowed he'd never refuse a request from anyone. So far his record was intact.

'Wouldn't mind giving a few tips to the lads taking

part, would you, Adam?' Bob asked with one of his biggest grins. 'Be a bit of an interval before the Final, you see, and everyone would be delighted to hear what you've got to say. Or you could just tell us all what it's like to play in the First Division at your age. Players you've met, saves you've made, training routines. Anything you like.'

Adam swallowed hard and said he didn't think that was quite in his line tonight, he wasn't prepared for it. But, somehow, beaming Bob persuaded him instead to answer a few questions from the players whose teams had been knocked out in earlier rounds. It wasn't much of an ordeal because they were all so deferential, and the answers were all so obvious he didn't have to search for them. Then, just when it was all flowing, Bob had to cut in because the Press photographer had arrived and they were ready for the Final.

'Good to see you again, Adam,' was the greeting from the cameraman, a self-confessed City supporter. 'Always seem to be taking your pic. these days, don't I?'

Another boost to his ego.

Feeling like a national celebrity at Wembley, he shook hands with each player before the Final kicked off. One of them, a thin-faced, intense boy call Billy, reminded him strongly of Carl whom he'd met with Jason at Riverside; and he experienced a momentary pang of guilt because since that encounter, when he was out on a training run, he hadn't dropped by to have a kick-around with them again. He hadn't exactly promised he would but he knew they'd be keen to keep up the contact. Perhaps he'd manage to see them one evening the following week.

The Final was an anti-climax. The favourites, who sported an unusual strip in brown-and-gold, were plainly affected by nerves and quickly gave away a couple of soft goals. Adam winced as he noted their goalkeeper's lack of positional sense: but then realised he ought not to display any partiality or criticism. The under-dogs, on the other hand, seemed to gain confidence with every pass and shot. They won easily, as easily as the 5–1 scoreline suggested.

As he handed over the handsome silver-and-wood plaque to the triumphant skipper it occurred to Adam that with a bit of luck he might be on the receiving end of a trophy this season – if City played at their peak and had the luck of the draw. In spite of his own success in getting into a First Division side so soon, he'd never won a medal of any kind as a footballer – yet.

'Well, Adam, we're all very grateful to you for coming out to Tanton this evening,' Bob Boscombe declared publicly, his smile radiating like a lighthouse. 'We all know how busy a life you and all the other City stars lead, so to give up your own time to watch young players in action is a very generous gesture. We thank you deeply for that. Now, we can't let you go without making a little gesture of our own. We'd like you to accept this gift as a memento of a very special occasion. I'm sure you'll find it most useful because, as you showed tonight, you have to do a lot of signing these days. Hope you like it – and hope you'll never use it to sign for any other club! So, best of luck to you and all the other City players, and thanks again.'

There was no need for him to make any reply because the applause was loud and long. All he had to do was wave his thanks – and then use his new silver-coloured pen to write the final autographs of the evening. It wasn't, he reflected, a bad note on which to end his first mission as City's newest and youngest ambassador.

Six

With what he felt sure was unerring accuracy, Adam hurled the ball down the gleaming channel, his delivery smoother than it had ever been. He sensed it was going to be a strike and he exulted, half-turning already to give a celebratory salute to his opponent. Karl Holliday, however, was watching impassively as if he didn't believe anything special was going to happen.

Karl was a good judge. At what seemed like the very last moment, the ball veered sharply off a straight line, clipping only one of the pins before plunging into the gutter; and that one falling pin dislodged only one more. Adam's lips tightened and he shook his head resignedly.

'I reckon you'd better give up throwing the ball out of defence in future,' Karl grinned. 'Your aim's gone to pot. The way you're going on you'd chuck it straight to the feet of their striker! Bang! And City are another goal down . . .'

Adam waited for the ball to be returned and then stowed it away on the shelf behind the desk where they could sit and tot up their scores. There didn't seem to be much point in computing his own achievements; they were minimal. Karl had won, as he himself was inclined to describe it, 'by the length of a street'.

But then, ten-pin bowling was one of Karl's favourite pursuits and it was his idea to spend the afternoon playing at the Top Bowl. In the weeks since Adam had taken over as first-team goalkeeper, he and Karl had become friendly and often spent their free afternoons together, although this was the first time they'd been ten-pin bowling. Karl's wife, Sharon, worked in a bank and as he preferred company to being on his own after training, they'd gone to the races a couple of times, been to the cinema, watched videos at Karl's home and even joined a snooker club.

Although only three years older than Adam, the restless, red-haired winger gave the impression he'd seen everything and done everything worth seeing and doing. Adam didn't mind that; in fact, he was learning quite a lot about life from his new friend. In any case, Karl had a sense of humour and always treated Adam as an equal.

'Got a girlfriend yet?' he asked as they changed out of the special lightweight bowling shoes.

Adam shook his head. 'Too busy with football and other things.'

Karl lifted an eyebrow. 'Well, how about that car you're supposed to be getting? Found anything yet? Plenty of ads in the papers, you know, if you're too lazy to tour the showrooms.'

Again Adam shook his head. 'Not that, either. Bit of a let-down, aren't I?'

'Well, Skipper, I reckon you're missing out on life's real excitements,' Karl remarked with a doleful expression. 'You need to start living it up a bit, Skips.'

Adam winced. Karl had this annoying habit of giving everyone a nickname and Skips or Skipper were the ones he favoured for Adam. But it seemed a bit juvenile to say he preferred to be known by his real name.

He wondered what Karl would say if everyone started to call him Hols? He must try it sometime, though he guessed that Karl would simply be amused and probably adopt the name gleefully.

'Expect I'm a bit of a loner, really,' Adam confessed. 'Goalkeepers usually are, you know. Last line of defence and all that. Rob says we've got to get used to relying just on ourselves.'

'Listen, mate, in my opinion you're getting to be too much under old Ouch's influence. Rob Heanor isn't God, you know. Doesn't even rate as high as Boss Fenn-ed-You-Off. You should do your own thing, Skips.'

'I do do my own thing,' Adam retorted. 'That's why I go for my daily run. Nobody orders me to do that. Look, if I can prove I'm fitter as a result of following my own schedule then that's bound to be in my favour. You never know, if that happens Rob Heanor might even get the sack for not doing his job properly!'

'Oh yeah, that's a thought. Good thinking. It'd do us all a power of good if we could get a replacement for Ouch. Then training might – might, mind you – become a pleasure again. A time to lie back and enjoy life.' He paused and then added: 'Well, while I have a go at that, I suppose I'd better run you home so you can go and run for yourself!'

In Karl's brilliant red BMW they were at Adam's home within ten minutes. Cars were a passion of Karl's and on a number of occasions he'd taken Adam to visit showrooms and second-hand dealers to investigate the potential of this model or that bargain. Although by now he had enough money to buy a second-hand car or put down a substantial deposit on a new one, Adam wasn't going to rush into it. In fact, he greatly enjoyed driving Zoe's Fiat – he believed it was a lucky car for him – and he hoped she'd sell it to him when she treated herself to a new one.

'Take care then. See you tomorrow. Don't forget, I'll score the goals to make up for the ones you let in at your end!'

That was one of Karl's favourite parting shots on the eve of a City match and Adam still hadn't come up with a suitable rejoinder.

His mother was just about to go out as he entered the house but she paused to ask him what he'd been up to: and, predictably, frowned when he said he'd been ten-pin bowling with Karl. Helen Skipsea was still thoroughly suspicious of her only son's new career which she viewed as frivolous. A footballer's career was short, so what sort of future would Adam have if he didn't obtain qualifications or experience for another job? Adam argued that he'd do so well in soccer that, when he finished playing, other good jobs would simply be offered to him.

'Will you be out long?' he asked her politely. 'I'm going out on my run as soon as I've changed.'

'You'd better wait a bit. Someone's phoning you back shortly.'

'Oh, who?'

'No idea. He wouldn't say. Just said it was important to talk to you today.'

Adam was irritated. He didn't like mysteries. Then it occurred to him that it could be the person who'd telephoned him that morning at the training ground. After all, he'd never heard from him again. 'What sort of guy was he – a journalist, d'you think? Or maybe someone wanting to cadge spare tickets?'

'Adam, it's not my custom to analyse other people's phone calls.'

'I'm not other people, I'm your son,' he said with

unnecessary waspishness.

His mother's expression, however, remained cool. 'If someone wants to tell me something, I'll listen. I'll even take notes in order to leave a message for you. But I will not cross-question a caller who simply says he'll call again. If I went in for that sort of thing every time you had a call you'd accuse me of interfering in your life. Or trying to find out what you're up to.'

'Sorry,' he muttered. He couldn't deny she was right.

'Right,' she went on briskly, 'then I'm on my way. I expect I'll be back within the hour if you're worried about when we're eating this evening.'

The last thing Adam wanted to do was to hang about aimlessly, but he decided he ought to wait until the caller rang again. He'd been lying on his bed for a good fifteen minutes and was just deciding that he really was wasting his time when the phone rang. Hurtling into his parents' bedroom, he snatched up the receiver.

'Is that Adam Skipsea?'

'Yes. Who is it?'

'Do you want your sister to go to jail on the most serious charge there is? Go to jail and stay there for the rest of her life?'

The voice was cool and had no discernible accent. Every word was clearly spoken but Adam couldn't believe what he'd heard.

'What – who –' He had no idea what to say.

'You heard what I said. I'm not going to repeat it,' the voice continued in the same businesslike tone. 'Jail is where your sister will go if you don't cooperate with us, if you don't do exactly what we tell you to. Understand?'

'No, of course I don't! What the hell's going on? Who are –'

'Then listen, Skipsea, listen. I'll only say this once: your sister's in deep trouble. You can get her out of it by doing exactly what we tell you to. In a few days' time you'll get another message with our instructions.'

'Look, what's Zoe –'

'Don't interrupt! Just listen. You can ask her about what she's done. Just do as you're told and everything will work out. One word of advice: tell no one, no one at all, about this. Otherwise Zoe will be the one to suffer, Zoe and the rest of your family.'

'You're just having a joke, aren't you?' said Adam, beginning to feel quite desperate. He couldn't really believe that one of his team-mates would carry out a practical joke like this; but it wasn't impossible. A situation like this couldn't be real.

'No joke, no joke at all,' the voice continued remorselessly. 'We'll prove that to you before the next phone call. Then you'll know this is no joking matter.'

The line went dead.

Adam heard a click and then buzzing, but it was some moments before he was able to replace the receiver. It wasn't a joke: he was sure of that now. The ice in the voice convinced him that the man, whoever he was, meant what he said. So that must mean that he was crazy, some kind of crank. Adam bit his lip. He hoped so. He hoped the whole thing was the warped idea of a lunatic who imagined he was sane.

No, it wasn't like that at all. The guy sounded completely sane, sane and deadly serious. Maybe it was a case of mistaken identity. Nothing to do with Zoe or anyone else in the Skipsea family.

Adam was already on his way to Zoe's bedroom to ask her what she knew about anything that could cause trouble for them, when he remembered that his sister was staying with her friend Hazel in Worcester for a couple of days. He would have telephoned her immediately if he'd known how to reach her; but he didn't know Hazel's surname and he had no idea at all of her whereabouts in Worcester. Instead, he returned to his own room and sank on the bed, trying feverishly to work out what was going on. Could Zoe really be in danger of going to jail? To jail for life? So far as he knew, there was only one crime that would be punished by a life sentence: and that was the crime of murder.

Adam swallowed hard. Zoe worked in an old people's home and there it was quite natural for residents to die. They didn't have much life expectancy when they arrived. Sometimes Zoe chatted about her old folk, about their amazing memories or peculiar habits, their obsessions and devotion to particular foods: their fads, in other words. Some of them she practically regarded as friends. Mrs Eastbrook, for instance, was 'just like I imagined a grandmother to be. She's lovely and kind and caring and you'd never think she was eighty-two'. Well, Zoe was kind and caring, too. It was utterly impossible to suppose she could be involved in murdering anyone at Seabright Villas.

No, the whole idea was nonsense. So what was really behind the telephone call? Had Zoe got herself involved in some other crime, something that would carry a severe sentence if you were caught? Adam quickly sorted through a few possibilities and came up with only one: drugs. He shook his head. Zoe simply wasn't the type to use or traffic in drugs. True, the Villas had its own mini-medical centre ('a proper mini-hospital,' Zoe called it) because prompt treatment was essential in any establishment that catered exclusively for the elderly. But hard drugs? Ridiculous.

It was also ridiculous to sit around trying to solve a mystery for which he didn't have a single clue. The entire conversation – no, not conversation; he had just been given a message – was incomprehensible. Until he could talk to Zoe there was no hope of understanding any of it. Adam decided he might as well get on with his ordinary life which meant going out on his daily run. Perhaps something useful might occur to him while he was concentrating on something else.

Once he'd changed into a tracksuit he began to relax. He thought of switching to a new route in order to keep his mind off the phone call. But familiarity won, and he was determined that this afternoon he'd improve on his best time. Records in this field weren't important to him but he thought it was always bene-ficial to have a target. In that way, too, he could explain to anyone he encountered and who wanted to detain him for a chat or an autograph that he simply had to keep on the move in order to maintain his club schedule. It sounded completely authentic for a professional sportsman, and it did the trick.

Usually, as he ran, Adam thought about the last game he'd played and went over all the incidents in which he'd been involved: free kicks, corners, low crosses, goalmouth scrambles. Could his reactions have been better? Should he have done this or that? Adam tried to put out of his mind any comments Ian Fenn or Rob Heanor had made in post-mortems either on the day itself or during the next training session. It was how he thought he'd performed that mattered because, often enough, neither manager nor coach had made any observation at all on a situation where Adam felt he had been at fault or not reacted quickly enough. But then, neither of them was a goalkeeper. They couldn't possibly feel as he did about all the finer points of making absolutely sure the ball was kept out of the net.

Now, as he left the house and crossed the Avenue, heading towards Prospect Hill, he tried to force himself to think about the following night's match against Watford, a team City held in high regard. Watford had a big, bustling, black centre-forward – a speciality of theirs, it seemed – and Adam knew he'd be in for a hard time at corners, free kicks or whenever he and Worrall, the centre-forward, believed there was a fifty-fifty ball on. Worrall's heading power was legendary and Adam hoped City's defenders would be able to cut out any crosses aimed towards the front of the box.

City needed to win this match, not only to improve their League position but to boost their confidence for the Cup-tie against RSV Antwerp the following week. That would be Adam's first European match and he was looking forward to it, not least because it would attract a lot of attention in the national Press; so if he did well, he'd probably get a good write-up. So far, his book of Press cuttings was mainly made up of local reports, apart from a few very brief mentions in tabloid Sunday papers.

He exchanged a friendly wave with Mrs Butterworth, a neighbour who used to give him a box of toffees every Christmas when he was a youngster (a present his mother promptly annexed in order to ration his supply of sweets). Then he cut through a narrow alley-way between detached houses and emerged at the top of the steep hill that would eventually bring him out opposite Endless Bank. The pavement was almost non-existent on the stretch beside an orchard which was protected by a wooden fence high enough to deter young raiders with designs on the apples and pears. At this time of day, before commuter traffic poured out of the city, it was a quiet area, for the steepness of the gradient deterred most casual walkers and joggers.

He heard the car only at the last moment, as the driver slickly changed gear and the noise of the engine rose sharply. The bang which followed was thunderous. Suddenly the fence beside Adam was quivering as if it had been shaken by a giant hand. Horrified, he swung round to see what had happened – and saw the car coming straight at him. It had struck the fence once, almost broadside, and rebounded; and now it was going to smash Adam into the next section of the fence a few metres further down the hill.

The car wasn't going to miss. In the split-seconds of terror before it reached him, Adam was certain he was going to die. In those awful moments he and the driver locked glances. And what Adam saw was blind determination – determination to drive the car straight through him as if he didn't exist. As he wouldn't exist when it hit him.

He couldn't run. There was nowhere to run to. The car swerved. At the last moment, the very last moment, it swerved. It struck the fence with a resounding bang that set it quivering again. But it missed Adam. He was still alive. It seemed hard to believe.

Adam's ordeal wasn't over. Having bounced away from the fence, the car slithered to a halt a few metres down the hill as the driver braked hard. Adam could hear him engaging gear and next moment, after a frantic wheel spin, the car was backing up towards him. This time, though, it wasn't being aimed at him.

He still hadn't decided which way to run when the car screeched to a halt beside him. Thrusting his head out of the window the driver yelled: 'Next time, we won't miss you, Goalie! Do as you're told and you and your sister will stay alive.'

Then, with another fierce spin of the wheels, the car roared away, down the slope and out of sight.

Adam tried to moisten his lips but his mouth was as dry as a sandbox and it was hard just to swallow. He looked at his watch but the time told him nothing about what had happened: only that it was approximately six minutes since he'd left home. The encounter with the car had lasted, what? half a minute, twenty seconds? He had no idea. Except that it was all over before he had time to think about anything except whether he would die – or survive.

Now, he tried to recall what he could of the incident. He still couldn't move. It was as if the onslaught had petrified him, turned him to stone.

Even before the driver had spoken he'd known it was a deliberate attempt to frighten him (not, as he'd first thought, to kill him). It was impossible to mistake the expression on the driver's face as the car arrowed towards him. He didn't think he'd ever forget the face, with its thin, stretched lips, narrowed eyes, wide nose. And the cap, a nondescript colour, a mixture of browns, pulled low on the forehead. Did the guy always wear it like that or was it to conceal his hair? Suddenly, he realised that someone else had been in the car, in the front passenger seat: but that person had turned his head away when the car reversed so that the driver could shout his message. It would be impossible to identify him.

The car itself was a Capri, red, shiny in places, battered elsewhere. Oldish model. But Adam hadn't noticed the number. In any case, a hit-and-run car like that probably didn't carry number plates. Or, if it did, they'd be false. That was the sort of thing that went on in the crime thrillers Adam occasionally read.

Gradually he began to feel alive again. He turned and studied the scars on the fence where the car struck it; the flecks of red paint contrasted with the strip of fresh wood gouged out when some projecting bit of metal had made contact. Without that last minute swerve, the car would have impaled him on the fence – or, more likely, driven him straight through it into the orchard. But, and this much he had to concede, the driver was undoubtedly skilful: a hit man who knew precisely how close to get to his victim without actually hitting him. The only mark he'd left on Adam was on his mind. A mark that time would never erase.

At last he moved away from the fence, breaking into a run, heading as usual down the hill on his familiar route. He could think as he ran, think about what he should do next.

Up to now, his only thoughts about the phone call had concerned Zoe and what she had done to set off such threats. He'd forgotten that the caller wanted something from him: that he was being ordered to follow instructions whenever they were issued. Adam had suggested that the man was joking. The answer to that had now been made forcefully apparent. The man had not been joking. The threat was real.

What did they want him to do?

As he tried to grapple with the question, a man wearing a blue trilby hat came out of a side-turning. He was swinging a walking-stick with evident pleasure. Because of what was on his mind Adam ducked away as if to avoid running into him.

'You all right?' the man asked him.

'Er, yeah – yeah, I think so,' Adam replied. For some reason the man seemed vaguely familiar to him but he couldn't quite place him. His mind was still whirling like a Catherine wheel.

'Well, if I were you, I'd take more care – make sure you don't run any risks,' remarked Blue Hat in a conversational manner. 'Can't be too careful these days, young feller.'

Adam nodded, not really listening; it was the sort of advice spectators were always giving him from behind his goal – when they were being polite. Then, with a wave of his stick, the man walked briskly away.

He realised that this was the first person he'd seen since the incident with the Capri. By sheer luck – because it couldn't be anything else – neither person nor vehicle had come in sight of them from the moment the Capri hit the fence until it disappeared down the hill. There had not been a single witness to the ferocious hit-and-run attack. Grazes on a fence were commonplace. So there'd be no point in drawing attention to them if he told anyone what had happened.

If he didn't do what they wanted then next time they might kill him. He had no doubt at all that they were capable of it. But what did they want from him?

Seven

Three minutes before half-time Watford scored the goal that had been threatening during a long spell of sustained pressure. Their free-running midfield player darted tantalisingly down the right flank, beating two defenders by a combination of pace and sorcery; then, just when it seemed certain he would float in a high cross, he hit a low ball just short of the near post.

It was one of those fifty-fifty balls that goalkeepers tend to hate. In normal circumstances Adam would have gone for it, confident he'd gather it before an opponent could flick it into the middle. This time he hesitated fractionally and fatally. Bishop, Watford's nippy striker, reached the ball with a split-second to spare and neatly hooked it clear of Adam's despairing arms and into the goalmouth for his partner to nod it contemptuously into the yawning net. It was some weeks since he'd put away an easier chance. The travelling fans with the yellow, black and red scarves celebrated ecstatically as Adam went to retrieve the ball.

That goal would, he knew, be put down to his error. And that was fair. He should have gone for the cross the moment he thought about it. As a junior, crosses to the near post had been one of his weaknesses. If you went for the ball and missed it then it was seventy-five per cent certain a goal would be the result. That, anyway, was the view of his first coach who went to great trouble to show him how to overcome the problem. Because Adam was a quick learner, as well as adaptable, he eventually became particularly adept at dealing with that kind of attack. Now, however, his concentration had wavered and his instinct for prompt action had vanished. Temporarily, he hoped. City were a goal down at home.

He tried to avoid looking towards the bench where Rob Heanor would be fulminating to Alex Hart or City substitutes about the setback. Ian Fenn was, for once, playing as an out-and-out striker and was too far upfield to drop back to remonstrate with his goalie. Adam would have had to endure his error in silence if it hadn't been for Ricky Gannon's comment.

'Should have cut that one out, son,' the central defender said, mildly enough. As the new team skipper, he was entitled to express his views publicly. Moreover, he was, in a way, helping to absolve another team-mate, Glen Quartley, one of the back four, from blame. Strictly speaking, Glen, who played on the left, should have closed Bishop down and so was partly at fault.

Adam wasn't in a position to argue. Just before the Watford midfielder began his dash down the wing, Adam had been thinking about something that had nothing whatsoever to do with football. And he couldn't recall that ever happening to him during a match since he became a professional player. He'd tried to put that phone call from the Capri Gang, out of his mind; but it was impossible. The menace of their threats couldn't be suppressed, they were constantly filtering into his consciousness whatever he was doing. And they wouldn't go away until he'd talked to Zoe and sorted things out from there. But Zoe wouldn't be home until the following evening. And now, because of his incompetence, City were losing.

Until that goal went in, City had been playing well enough to score at least three times themselves, only to be thwarted by the brilliance of the Watford goalkeeper or the misfortune of their own strikers in front of goal.

Watford's confidence, however, had been growing and the pressure they'd been exerting before the goal was scored didn't stop; they sensed that another goal before half-time could clinch the match for them. From the re-start, Bishop intercepted a careless pass meant for Ian Fenn and began a mazy, penetrative run that took him right to the edge of the penalty area, where he slipped the ball inside the hesitant full-back, Glen Quartley. Even as Glen was turning, the winger he thought he'd been marking pounced and with rare aplomb, flicked the ball upwards and across the goalmouth for Worrall to head it home again.

Ricky Gannon, who'd decided to attach himself to Worrall like a shadow, actually rose first for the ball, just as Adam decided he, too, must go for it. Antonio Worrall possessed the invaluable knack of being able to climb and hover in the air before directing his header wherever he chose: it was all due to impeccable timing. He was just reaching the perfect altitude when Adam arrived to collect the ball: but because he was now impeded by Ricky, Adam had to try to punch the ball clear instead of catching it. And punch it with his left fist. And because that punch had to be delivered over Ricky's shoulder it wasn't very successful. The ball ricocheted from the Watford striker's left ear and would have entered the net after one bounce by the right-hand post if Simon Rokefield hadn't hurriedly hooked it over the dead-ball line for a corner.

'You owe me a pint for saving your life there,' Simon told Adam as they awaited the kick. Adam couldn't argue with that. He had committed another blunder, although there was some excuse for this one. He caught a glimpse of Ian Fenn, loitering at the edge of the box, and the frown on the manager's face he sensed was aimed at him. Thankfully, the kick was unproductive, Ricky rocketing the ball to safety with a powerful header.

Adam's confidence seemed to have evaporated. He was feeling distinctly jittery, worrying now about the next raid and how he would cope with it. Watford, still determined if possible to add to their lead before the interval, attacked next down the right flank and this time it was Antonio Worrall who produced the swinging centre. Adam, who'd been pleading silently with the ref. to blow his whistle for half-time, could see no danger for his defence in this move: but surely it couldn't be as innocuous as it looked. The tallest of Watford's midfielders was racing in from the left but, really, he had no hope of meeting the cross. All the same, he was a distraction, Adam took his eye off the ball as he came out for it: and next moment it was spinning off his fingertips, straight towards the in-rushing midfielder.

Luckily for City, the Watford player was so astonished to find the ball coming at him that he completely misjudged his header, sending the ball soaring over the bar. Adam, rolling his eyes upwards in relief, raced to collect it from the ball boy. He couldn't bear to look at his fellow-defenders. He could imagine their reactions to his latest fumble only too vividly.

'Get a grip, Skips!' Ricky told him fiercely. Adam

was too distraught to notice that the centre-back had picked up the nickname that Karl had invented. What on earth was going to happen next time he went for the ball? He remembered that one of his coaches had likened goalkeeping errors to falling off a horse: 'you've got to get back on that horse as fast as possible so your confidence isn't destroyed – and the same thing applies to goalkeeping, you've got to get hold of that ball and control it, dominate it. You don't hang back and hope it won't come near you.' Sound advice, Adam was sure. But he still stared apprehensively down the pitch, watching the ball intently and praying that City would attack unceasingly and get on top in this game.

In fact, a run by Ian Fenn ended when he was dispossessed on the edge of the Watford box and, two kicks later, the ball was back in Adam's hands. This time, though, it had been turned back to him deliberately by Ricky Gannon who'd intercepted a long pass to Bishop. Ricky's aim was to re-inject some confidence into his goalkeeper. 'Yours,' he called out as he side-footed the ball towards Adam who was very grateful indeed for the chance to cradle it in his arms again. It was at that moment that the ref. signalled half-time and so it looked to many spectators as though Ricky's gesture was really a time-wasting device.

Rob Heanor had no illusions of any kind about Adam's performance in this match. 'What the hell's got into you, Adam?' he demanded even before they reached the dressing-room. When Ian was playing in a match, Rob took over the role of 'manager' and delivered the half-time pep talk, firing the darts at those players who'd been at fault in the first forty-five minutes.

Adam didn't know what to say. He'd never seen the coach look so angry, and he knew that anger was justified. But how could he explain that his mind had wandered because of personal worries? That wouldn't be acceptable as an excuse. But it would be a reason to drop him from the team. He shrugged with theatrical emphasis, spread his hands wide and then slumped into his usual place on the bench in the dressing-room.

'You were dithering like an old woman on a pedestrian crossing in the rush-hour,' Rob accused him. 'You're bloody lucky we're not three goals down, instead of just the one you gave 'em with both hands! I thought you'd had a brainstorm or were paralysed or something. What were you playing at, eh?'

'I just can't explain it,' Adam told him, reaching for a cup of tea.

'I should think you can't – it's beyond belief,' Heanor said scathingly, staring at Adam as though he were some kind of freak; it was one of his most disconcerting ploys when chastising a player. 'What were you thinking about, eh?'

'Nothing.' Then, hurriedly: 'I mean, the game, what was going to happen next, where the ball was going –'

'Rubbish! Bloody nonsense! That's just what you weren't doing, anybody could see that.' Rob paused and looked round the changing-room. The Boss was deep in conversation with Alex Hart who, simultaneously, was checking on a muscle strain that Simon Rokefield complained was still bothering him. Glen Quartley was listening intently to Ricky's views on defensive play on the edge of the box. 'Come on, then,' Rob resumed, swinging back to face Adam at close range. 'What were you thinking about? Some girl?'

'Course not! I wouldn't think about that in the middle of a game.' Adam's denial was emphatic enough to convince Heanor he was on the wrong track. The irony of the situation (which the coach naturally wasn't aware of) was that he had been thinking about a girl: his sister Zoe – and the appalling problem that had suddenly invaded their lives.

'Well, don't let it happen again, understand? Otherwise you'll be out of this team faster than you got into it.' Rob could think of no other way of dealing with this uncharacteristic lapse than to utter the sort of threat that brought most players to their senses pretty quickly. 'Concentration is as important as breathing. If you give up on either of 'em you're dead!'

Rob stood up and walked away to have a word with the Boss, now enjoying a gentle massage of his calf muscles from Alex. Adam sagged in his seat and took a long drink of the sugary tea. Karl Holliday gave him a sympathetic grin and said softly: 'Don't worry, Skips. He'll forget all about it – if we win.'

As the players jogged out for the second half, Ian Fenn put his arm on Adam's shoulder. 'Forget the first half, Adam,' he murmured in his usual relaxed manner. 'Just keep a clean sheet in the second. OK?'

'Sure, Boss,' Adam replied automatically. But he wondered what was really on Fenn's mind. If City lost this match, he was sure he'd be dropped.

The crowd behind the Cato Street goal greeted him enthusiastically when he tossed his cap and gloves into the back of the net and took up his position; they'd always been among his best supporters and were one of the reasons why he usually preferred to defend this end in the second half of a match. It was where he'd pulled off what he regarded as the finest save of his career, a reflex response to a header at point-blank range from a Liverpool striker who played regularly for Scotland. On that occasion he'd even managed to cling on to the ball. It strengthened him to think about it now.

Watford, eager for the three points that would help them to climb into the top half of the Division, began again where they'd left off and within moments Adam was racing off his line to foil Worrall who was pursuing a lofted pass from just inside the City half. Although he immediately threw the ball out to Simon he felt he was in command of his area again. Taking decisive action was always an aid to concentration, according to Rob Heanor. Soon afterwards, the visitors won a corner on the right, conceded unnecessarily by Ricky, and this time Adam took the ball cleanly with both hands when Worrall tried to head it into the net after a flick-on from the near post. His fans behind the goal cheered and clapped vociferously. After the ball had been punted up towards the other end Adam gave his supporters an appreciative wave. They were definitely a boost to his morale when he most needed it.

Although plainly frustrated by their inability to add to their lead, Watford made no attempt to close down the game and simply defend in depth: they believed they had the measure of City. That was very nearly true except that they hadn't allowed for the genius of Ian Fenn.

With the sort of superb pass that had first brought him to the attention of City's chief scout during an otherwise humdrum non-League match, Glen Quartley fed Karl Holliday right on the touchline and still inside his own half of the pitch. Karl's acceleration was impressive and the retreating full-back stumbled as City's winger turned to go one way and then zipped past him on the other side. Although he had a clear path ahead of him for the moment, Karl took everyone by surprise by firing the ball hard and low towards Ian, now arriving on the edge of the box. The two defenders attending him were marginally slow in sensing the danger as Ian pulled the ball down with one foot and then, with the other, chipped it over the head of the nearer opponent. Before the player could turn, Ian seized possession again and then drove the ball fiercely past the goalkeeper into the top of the net.

It was by any standards a brilliant, breath-taking goal, one that deserved to win a Cup Final or a show-piece international. Yet in this match it merely brought the scores level. As his fellow goalkeeper shook his head in disbelief and went to retrieve the ball, Adam experienced a surge of relief. At least City weren't going to lose the match as a result of his original blunder – that is, so long as he didn't concede another goal. With just a touch of luck, Watford might be demoralized by that dramatic example of Fenn magic and cave in for City to win. Well, he could hope . . .

As it turned out, Bishop now seemed determined to emulate Ian Fenn by scoring a memorable goal, for whenever he managed to get hold of the ball he stuck to it, striving to outwit City's defence entirely on his own. Ricky became ever more agitated as the blond midfielder switched this way and that, turned in half circles, swung his foot teasingly over the ball, darted forward, edged sideways, even stood with one foot on the ball, inviting a tackle. Sometimes he lost the ball quite quickly, at others he retained control so long that the home fans began to howl their disapproval of Bishop for hogging the ball and their disappointment with City's defence for not taking it off him.

Ten minutes from full-time, however, Bishop got more or less what he wanted. In possession once more, he dallied on the edge of the box, tapping the ball from foot to foot before unexpectedly making a dash for-ward: and at that precise moment, Sim Rokefield powered in to make a crunching tackle. Bishop collapsed in a heap. It was Antonio Worrall and the other Watford players with a close-up view of the incident who screamed for a penalty. Sensibly, Bishop simply lay prone until he could receive treatment from the physio. The referee gave the impression he didn't know what decision to make and he made a point of consulting his linesman while players and fans alike argued amongst themselves.

Then, to the fury of the home crowd, the referee raced back to the penalty area, pointing to the spot.

Adam swore and then gritted his teeth. A penalty was the last thing he wanted to face. Though his record was quite good in all matches (twenty-six penalty shots saved out of fifty-five) it was so easy to be made to look a total idiot: you dived one way and the ball flashed into the opposite corner of the net. Or, worse, you half-saved the shot but the ball then spun under your body and over the line. On the other hand, a spectacular save was rarely forgotten by anyone. Reputations had been built on keeping out penalty kicks. Tonight, it was his one opportunity to atone for giving Watford their goal.

Bishop had miraculously recovered all his faculties following the physio's ministrations and was preparing to take the kick himself. Adam recalled that, in the pre-match briefing based on reports by City's chief scout, Bishop usually struck the ball to the goalie's left. He would, Adam reflected, thinking of his own alleged weakness, he would. But Adam had his own method of determining what a penalty-kicker might do. However much he might try to disguise it, the kicker invariably glanced, if only for a split-second, at the spot he was really going to aim at. Usually he did so just as he was about to start his run. In any case, after that there was no chance whatsoever for the goalkeeper to rely on further guesswork.

Bishop walked away after re-placing the ball on the spot and then turned, flicking a look at Adam's right-hand post. Initially, he appeared to saunter and then, in no more than a couple of strides, reached the ball, kicking with his left foot. Unlike many goalkeepers, Adam never moved until the ball had been struck. Now, sure of which way it was going, he leapt. And grabbed the ball at arm's length no more than a foot above the turf. And kept hold of it as he fell.

The roar that greeted the save was thunderous. But Adam scarcely heard it. He was already being mobbed by every City player who could reach him although he was still clutching the ball. Bishop had followed up, though there was nothing in it for him any more. He sensed – and he was absolutely right – that Watford's last chance of winning the match had gone.

Adam punted the ball joyfully upfield and then savoured his triumph. He really had made up for his first-half lapses, so surely there could be no thought of dropping him for the next match, the Antwerp Cup-tie. In the second half he hadn't made a semblance of a mistake and the save from the penalty kick ought to win him plenty of credit marks from Rob Heanor, especially as he'd anticipated Bishop's change of direction. When the final whistle blew, he could feel that he'd done as much as the Boss himself to save City a point.

Others thought so, too. 'Terrific, Skips! Kept us alive,' Karl enthused, slapping him on the back so force-fully he practically knocked him off balance as they hurried up the tunnel to the changing-room. 'Well done, son. You sure improved on your first-half per-formance,' was Rob Heanor's more sober assessment. The Boss was glowing: 'Brilliant effort, Adam. If you can keep up that sort of form I'll be fighting off the offers for you!'

The level of euphoria in the bath gave Adam some inkling of what it might be like to be part of a Cup-winning team. It was Ian's goal, just as much as Adam's save, that had lifted the squad's spirits, coupled with the fact that, because of the arrangement of fixtures in the smaller First Division, they would all have a rare Saturday off. Their next match would be the Cup-tie in Belgium a week hence against RSV Antwerp and everyone seemed to be looking forward to that, partly because it would enable them to enjoy a change of routine, coupled with some foreign travel.

After a couple of unwinding drinks in the players' lounge, Adam accepted the offer of a lift home from Karl who, true to form, was bubbling with plans, both for the weekend and when they were in Belgium. 'Some good racing at Newbury on Saturday, and I've got word of a sure thing, straight from the trainer's mouth – which is better than the horse's mouth in the best racing circles! So we ought to go and fill our pockets with lovely loot. Then, in Antwerp we'll do a tour of the motor showrooms to see what's new in Europe. Can get some great bargains over there, you know.'

Adam didn't know, but he was prepared to take Karl's word for it. When Antwerp was mentioned it crossed his mind that over there he could escape all contact with the Capri Gang. He could forget them and then life would return to normal. With a bit of luck, by the time he returned home they'd have forgotten about him, too. He knew he'd enjoy Karl's company on Saturday, and the change of scene. All the same, he felt a touch of guilt about fixing up to go to the races: really, he ought to take the opportunity to attend a top League match and learn something from watching other goalkeepers in action. But he didn't think his team-mates would be sympathetic to that idea.

'Pick you up after an early breakfast – might as well make the most of our Saturday off,' Karl promised. 'See you, Skips.'

'See you, Karl.' Adam still couldn't bring himself to use a nickname of his own invention.

His parents were already in bed but he was relieved to see there were no messages on the pad beside the phone. For all her complaints about her family's behaviour, his mother was meticulous in noting down every call. So he could be confident the Capri Gang hadn't rung.

It didn't occur to Adam that they would be aware that he was playing in a night match and so would be out of reach. He was still on a mild high so he made himself a hot drink and then watched a favourite video film about an American high school kid who had the craziest adventures.

He slept as soundly as he always did after a match and it needed his mother's most persuasive touch – a fierce shaking of his right shoulder – to awaken him just before eight the following morning.

'What – what time is –' he tried to ask.

'Never mind the time, Adam! Go and answer the phone. Use the one in the bedroom. This man says it's a matter of life and death.'

Adam sat up, aghast. 'But who is it?'

His mother flung him his towelling robe. 'Don't waste time on stupid questions. If somebody rings you at this hour it must be important. So just go and answer it.' Then she turned and marched out of the room.

He had no doubt at all who was ringing him. He dreaded picking up the receiver and hearing that chilling voice. But he had to do it: he had to hear what they wanted.

He had to clear his throat more than once before he could speak. And then it was only, 'Hello.'

'Adam Skipsea?' It was that voice.

'Ye – es.'

'Listen carefully. I will not repeat this. Your sister will be home tonight. Say the name 'Lancaster' to her. Tell her we know all about it. Everything will come out in the open unless you do what we want. *Everything*.' There was a momentary pause. 'You've got to do what we want next week – next week. You'll get your instructions on Sunday.'

There was another pause and Adam found his voice. 'But, listen, I –'

Then he heard the click as the receiver was replaced at the other end.

'Oh God,' was all he could say. As he made his way back to his own room, his knees felt weak, as if they might give way.

'Have you finished, Adam?' he heard his mother calling out from the bottom of the stairs. 'I want to make a call myself.'

'Oh, yes, thanks.' He realised she could easily have listened to his call on the extension: but her question indicated that she hadn't. He found he was sweating now.

'Was it important, then?' She was still there.

'Well, sort of . . .' he fenced.

'Well, it's your business, not mine, I take it. Look, there's some breakfast on the table if you want it.'

'Not – not just now, Mum.'

Adam didn't think he'd ever feel like eating again.

Eight

By the time Zoe returned home early that evening, Adam had worked out what he should say and what he should do. For much of an agonising morning he'd thought about confiding in Karl, the person he supposed he would call his closest friend. But he still couldn't imagine what the Capri Gang wanted him to do for them and so there was really nothing to be gained from discussing his problem with Karl. His first priority was to talk to Zoe.

When the Fiat pulled into the drive, Adam was in the house on his own, his mother having gone to a business seminar at a local hotel and his father suffering a British Rail delay somewhere near Plymouth. His sister's smile, when she caught sight of him, was radiant. She'd had her hair cut shorter than usual and highlighted. She seemed to have taken a mass of luggage with her and, automatically, he gave her a hand with her cases.

'Hey, who's been making the headlines, then?' she greeted him.

'What?' His heart suddenly lurched.

'Saw a piece in the *Telegraph* this morning about you making a stupendous save – I think that's the word – from a penalty kick. The reporter said you saved

City a valuable point. Good stuff, Adam.'

'It was tremendous, not stupendous.' He dumped a second case on her bed.

'Zoe, I've got to ask you something important, *very* important. I'm not prying or anything but, well, something very odd is going on. And it involves you, I think.'

The smile had been replaced by a wary look and she began to play with a ring on the small finger of her left hand. 'Go on, then,' she said in a surprisingly firm voice. 'What did you want to ask?'

'Does the name Lancaster mean anything to you?'

'Oh God,' she breathed, sinking down on the end of her bed. 'Who told you?'

Adam shook his head. 'Can't tell you that because I don't know. But something is going on, isn't it? Zoe, you've just got to tell me.'

'I can't tell you anything,' she shot back. 'There's nothing to tell. It's all – over and done with.'

'Zoe, it isn't over! No way. I'm being threatened.'

'You can't be! Who by?'

'I've just told you, I don't know. This guy rang up.'

'Rang where? Here? At your Club? Rang you?'

Adam was about to lose his temper. 'Look, Zoe, I'm not making this up! This guy phoned up here and told me I've got to cooperate or else. All because of something you know about – or somebody called Lancaster. Fact is, he's rung more than once. The latest was this morning, early. I was asleep and Mum took it.'

'Mum knows?' Zoe was wide-eyed now and utterly dismayed.

He shook his head again. 'She just woke me up and handed the call over. I haven't said a word to her about it. How can I? I don't know anything. What's going on, Zoe? You've got to tell me.'

'I just can't, Adam. It's impossible. It's too personal.'

She was biting her lip furiously. 'It's all over now, I promise. Nothing can change what happened. I can't tell you anything because it's to do with work. So I'm not the only one who's involved. That's why nobody must say a word about it to anybody. It's too dangerous.'

Adam was now standing right over her, wanting to shake some understanding into her. 'Don't you realise other people do know about it? That's why I'm being threatened! If I don't do what they want, you could go to jail for life. That's what they said. For it to be as bad as that somebody must have died. Zoe, has something happened at the Villas?'

She was ashen. 'I can't talk about it, Adam, not even to you. Not yet. I'll have to talk to Mark first.'

'Mark Kelleher, you mean? Your boss?'

'Look, whatever else happens, you're not to say anything about this to Mum,' she told him in a fierce whisper as though Helen Skipsea were straining to overhear their conversation at that very moment. 'Promise me, Adam, promise me you won't tell her!'

Before Adam could answer, the telephone rang.

They looked at each other in disbelief. Adam's nerves felt as if they'd been shredded; a phone call at this moment couldn't be anything else but ominous. And Zoe was affected by his patent dread of what he might hear when he answered it.

'It's not this man who's been ringing you, is it?' she asked tremulously.

Adam licked his dry lips. 'It shouldn't be. He told me he'd ring on Sunday.'

The phone continued to ring.

'Well, you'll have to answer it,' she told him. 'Could be Dad or Mum.'

It didn't occur to him to tell Zoe that she should

answer it. Making his way slowly into their parents' bedroom hoping the caller would get tired of waiting and ring off, Adam reached for the receiver as though it were a poisoned dart.

'Hello,' he said faintly in a voice he would never have recognised as his own.

The caller had nearly the same problem. 'Adam? Is that Adam?'

His relief was enormous. It wasn't that voice. For the moment, it was all that mattered. 'Yes, yes it is. Adam Skipsea. Who's that?'

'Oh, great. Glad it's you, Adam. Thought you might be out. It's Jason – you know, Jason Carter. We met when you came and had a kick-in with Carl and me on the Youth Club pitch at Riverside. Remember? Just after you'd got into City's team against Everton.'

'Oh, yeah. I remember.' He was finding it hard to adjust to someone so different from the caller he'd feared.

'Look, I was wondering, Adam, if you'd like another game? You did say I could phone you up, said your number was in the book. So, well . . . I know City don't have a match on Saturday so I thought you might manage it then, or Sunday. Sunday morning would be great.'

'Can't manage Sunday. Sunday's impossible.' Adam was beginning to recover his balance; but the mention of Sunday disturbed him again.

'Oh, yeah, right. I understand, Adam. I suppose, well, Saturday then?'

'Sorry Jason. I'm fixed up on Saturday as well. I mean, just because City haven't a game it doesn't mean I have nothing to do.'

'Oh yeah, right.' Jason sounded utterly crestfallen but Adam was in no mood to sympathize with him.

'Well, perhaps some other time, Adam . . .'

'It'll have to be, Jason. Sorry, but this is a bad time for me. Look, I'll drop by when I can, O K?'

'Right, Adam. See you then. Oh, and best of luck in Antwerp next week. Hope you have a great game.'

Adam replaced the receiver and slowly walked back to Zoe's bedroom. She was still sitting on the bed in a trance-like state but some of her normal colour seemed to return when he told her: 'Wasn't him. One of my – the team's supporters. Just a coincidence.'

Zoe stood up. 'I'm going to have a bath. I need one.'

He stared at her. 'You can't do that now! We've got things to talk about, things to sort out. I told you –'

'Adam, there's not a thing we can do now. You said yourself this man's going to phone you on Sunday. Until he does ring we've no idea what he wants. Have we?'

Dumbly, Adam shook his head. He had no idea whether he was thinking straight or not. He didn't know what to think.

'Well, then, we've got to wait until then, see what happens. He may not ring at all. Tomorrow, I'll have a chance to talk things over with Mark, see what he says. I can't do anything, really, until I've talked to him. Adam, you've just got to understand that. For my sake.'

The interruption caused by Jason's phone call had given Zoe breathing space so she was calm and thinking logically.

But, for Adam, nothing had changed. He was still fearful of what was going to happen to him, to both of them.

Zoe gave him a quick kiss on the cheek. 'Try not to worry, Adam, please. I'm sure things will work out all right. It won't be as bad as you think.'

For once in his life, he didn't believe her.

Nine

By noon on Sunday Adam was still waiting for the telephone to ring. Twice, when it did ring and he darted into the study to snatch up the receiver, the calls were for his father who then grinned and remarked as he went to take them: 'This girl must be really special to have you on edge like this. Why don't you put yourself out of your misery and phone her instead? I won't worry about the phone bill just as long as she doesn't live in California!'

It was his utter helplessness that was really getting on Adam's nerves. Even when his goal was under siege and the ball was bobbing around tantalisingly, he could always make the decision to charge off his line to try to collect it. Here, all he could do was to wait, wait, wait. He'd got up early because he hadn't slept well and what he wanted most was to go for his daily run; but he daren't allow his mother to take the call for him because she was capable of saying anything to anyone, in spite of her assertion that she didn't interrogate those who rang members of her family. The sports pages of the Sunday papers, normally a source of prolonged fascination to Adam, failed to grip him. His music was no solace, and he almost smashed the headphones when he hurled them against the wall of his bedroom after discovering that the latest call was still not for him.

His one consolation was that no one fought him to get to the phone first because his father, claiming always to be off-duty on a Sunday, would only answer when he knew it was for him and was likely to be important. His mother had left for yet another committee meeting, and Zoe, too, had gone out, ostensibly to 'see a mate,' but, Adam supposed, really to make contact with Mark Kelleher.

Then, just as he'd decided to make something to eat, the phone rang again: and this time it was for him. He recognised the voice, with its chillingly calm, impersonal tone, as soon as the man asked if it was Adam Skipsea speaking.

'Listen very carefully and don't interrupt,' the voice went on. 'It's about the Antwerp match. You've got to lose it. You've got to make sure City lose.'

'You're crazy!' Adam gasped. 'I can't make the team lose. It's just not on, no way.'

'I said listen, Skipsea! No interruptions. I tell you this, if City don't lose then your sister will go to jail for life.' There was a pause but Adam sensed it was for effect. In any case, he had no idea what to say. 'It'll be easier than you think. If Antwerp aren't winning then all you've got to do is give them a penalty kick. That penalty kick will be taken by their Number 9. He will shoot to your left – your left, remember. You will jump to the right. It will all look quite natural.'

He stopped again and this time Adam realised he was expected to make a response. But his mind was whirling. He didn't know what to challenge first. Whatever he said, though, would be of no consequence. Of that he was certain.

'How can I be certain I'll be able to give them a

penalty? I mean, the way I knock a player over or something?' It sounded feeble but it was what came to mind.

'How you do it is up to you. You're the professional player. Just make certain they *do* get a penalty if Antwerp aren't winning.'

'Look, I've told you, there's no way I can guarantee to give them the match. It's just impossible.'

The pause this time was a fraction longer. Adam wondered if the man was re-thinking the situation. He began to hope he would realise the whole scheme was crazy and call it off. He should have known how vain such hopes were.

'If Antwerp do not win then the evidence of the crime committed by your sister will be given to the police. If you fail us, your sister will go to jail for life. If you make sure Antwerp win you will never hear from us again.'

Adam expected the phone to be put down at that point but it wasn't. His caller was waiting for him to say something. And one question came to the surface in the maelstrom of his mind.

'What's she done? What crime's she supposed to have committed?'

'Ask her,' was the clipped reply, and then the receiver went down.

He couldn't think what to do next. He had to talk to someone. But Zoe, the one person he needed to talk to, wasn't there; she'd return soon, he was sure, but until she did he'd have to keep everything bottled up. His parents were the last people he could confide in. He thought fleetingly of Karl Holliday. They'd had a good time at the races, in spite of the failure of 'the certainty of the day', as Karl described the tip he'd been given. Adam's worries surfaced several times but somehow he'd managed to shrug off Karl's inquiries. No, it would be hopeless to involve Karl now. After all, Karl was a member of the team Adam had been ordered to sabotage.

'You look really down in the dumps,' his father remarked cheerfully as Adam returned to the sitting-room intending to try and absorb himself in the papers again. 'Fancy going down to the pub for a swift half or two? If we're out of the house I can't take any more phone calls, can I?'

Even in his present state of despair, Adam couldn't miss the irony of that comment. 'I don't think so, thanks, Dad. Not really in the mood. I am pretty hungry, though. D'you think we could start lunch?'

'Oh sure, if you want to. Your Mum said not to wait for her, anyway, because that meeting could drag on. She's made a lasagne and it should be ready by now. Look, you go ahead, Adam. Don't think I could manage more food yet after that belated breakfast.'

So Adam had a solitary meal, the last thing he needed because his thoughts inevitably focused on one subject: the Cup-tie in Antwerp. After the episode with the Capri driver he had no doubt whatsoever that the gang threatening him meant every word they said. He knew that if he didn't obey their orders in Belgium, Zoe would suffer and, through her, the whole Skipsea family would suffer. What was he going to do?

He chewed on a strip of pasta without tasting it, and tried to work out some possibilites. He could for instance, declare himself unfit so City would have to play someone else in goal. It shouldn't be too difficult to fake an injury – a pulled muscle, severe backache, even a cut hand (and he could now, quite coolly, con-template 'accidentally' stabbing himself with a knife or something so that when Alex Hart examined the wound in City's treatment room, it would look perfectly authentic). Jake Keedwell would be delighted to get back his old place in the team.

Adam's spirits rose fleetingly as he decided he probably could get away with it because neither Rob Heanor nor Ian Fenn would ever imagine that he would deliberately exclude himself from the team: it was unheard of for any player who was young, fit and ambitious. But then, on reflection, he knew it wouldn't work. If he didn't cooperate and concede a penalty to ensure a victory for the home side then all the gang's planning would come to naught. He would be held responsible, and Zoe would finish up in jail. He had to play at Antwerp.

Was there any hope of salvation? Well, he supposed there was a faint chance that he might be dropped. After all, he'd made those horrendous blunders in the Watford match so the Boss might decide to leave him out at Antwerp just to make the point that he expected consistency in his goalkeeper. The Cup they were playing for wasn't one of the leading European competitions and not many hearts would be broken if City didn't get to the next round. On the other hand, the club was keen to register some success this season and any international trophy that could be put on display for the supporters was worth having. Therefore the Boss would always want to play his strongest team: and, at present, that team would include Adam Skipsea.

The other possibility that might work in his favour was that RSV would be too strong for them. No one seemed to know much about the Belgian side and because they were in the equivalent of a lower division in their own country the local sportswriters and City supporters were tending to write them off, suggesting that City should get through the tie without too much difficulty. Yet form upsets were commonplace in European matches: and City had very little recent experience of playing matches abroad.

His mind still racing, Adam wandered into the kitchen with his plate in search of something else to eat. He was delighted to discover a homemade plum pie. Raiding the freezer to add some strawberry-flavoured ice-cream, he let his hopes build up for a comfortable home victory. For all he knew, RSV might suddenly have discovered a couple of star players who would inspire the rest of the side to produce a scintillating performance. If they raced into a 3–0 lead, say, then City would surely feel the game was beyond them and give up. Then he wouldn't have to draw attention to himself by conceding an obvious penalty – and missing the ball when the kick was taken. If all went well with RSV in the early stages, he could perhaps help things along by fumbling a catch or failing to clear the ball in a mêlée in the goalmouth. Surely it wouldn't matter to the Capri Gang how RSV won, just as long as they did win.

Then, sooner than he'd expected, Zoe returned. Hearing the car in the drive he hurried out to intercept her.

'They've phoned!' he told her in a low voice. 'We've got to talk, Zoe.'

She nodded. Adam saw that she looked as strained as when he'd told her about the first call. In spite of his own anguish, he did feel a deep sympathy for her plight, whatever had caused it.

'Mum could be back any minute and I don't want her barging in on us,' Adam went on. 'And Dad's around, too. He even suggested he and I should go down to the pub! So it's quite possible he could have the idea of taking us all out to afternoon tea or something equally daft.'

Zoe thought for a moment and then said: 'OK, get in the car. We'll drive down to the river and park by the weir bridge. Nobody'll bother us there.'

It was a short journey to the river and they didn't talk until Zoe parked the Fiat in one of the few remaining spaces.

'So what does he want, then, this man who's been ringing you up?' she asked in a crisp, businesslike voice, though the way in which she was twisting the ring on her little finger betrayed her anxiety. 'He still wants something, does he?'

Adam nodded. 'He wants me to throw the match in Antwerp on Tuesday night, that's all! I've got to make sure RSV win and then everything'll be all right – he says. Zoe, I can't –'

'– and if you don't?' she cut in.

'If I don't, he'll tell the police about whatever you've done,' Adam said flatly. 'And my career will be over, that's certain.'

She frowned. 'But why? I thought you said it was me they're after.'

'Because they'll get their revenge on me as well, I know they will. They're that type. Look, they nearly killed me just after they'd phoned the first time. A guy in a car deliberately drove at me, just missing me by an inch! They said that was to back up their threats, to show they mean business. Zoe, they're killers!'

His sister leaned back against the door and studied him, working out what to say. 'If you were to do what they want, and let this Belgian team win, what difference would it make to you? No – think about it, Adam!' She hesitated, and then added: 'Would it really matter all that much?'

He'd been ready to explode when he heard the first question. Instead, he bit his lip and examined the situation from as many angles as he could.

'I'd feel terrible, absolutely terrible,' he admitted eventually. 'I mean, it's my job to stop goals, not give 'em away. I don't think I'd ever be able to look my mates in the eye again if I threw a match. Even if they didn't suspect what I'd done, I'd know, wouldn't I? And I'd never be able to forget it, not as long as I live. Zoe, we're talking about my career, you know, a career I've only just started out on.'

She reached out to put a hand on his knee. 'I know, Adam, I do understand how you feel. But, well, it is only a game of football, isn't it? It's not life or death or anything like that.'

Adam exploded. 'Football's everything to me, Zoe! Everything. I've just said, it's my career, my life. I can't give it up just because some rotten crooks want to fix a match. I wouldn't be able to live with myself ever again. I'd feel dead inside. It'd kill me!'

Zoe closed her eyes and tried to bring some sanity to the situation. Until now, she hadn't quite realised just how much football did mean to him. Sport to her had always been little more than a bit of fun; she'd simply never seen it in the serious light that her brother viewed it. Lately, she'd been too wrapped up in her own affairs even to realise that Adam had launched himself on a successful career.

'I'm sorry, Adam, really sorry,' she admitted. 'I wasn't thinking properly. But just listen a minute. It is only one match they're talking about, isn't it? Not even a League match in England, just a fairly unimportant Cup match in another country? So City won't lose any promotion points or anything like that, will they?'

'I know that but –'

'Hang on! Please. All I'm saying is, if it is a sort of minor match, your career won't depend on it. I mean, nobody'll suspect anything if you – help me. If I went to prison think what that would do to Mum and Dad – and you.'

'But what have you done, Zoe? What's happened? I've got to know.'

She nodded slowly. 'I know, I know. You're entitled to that after the way things have turned out. I'm sorry, Adam, truly sorry that you've been dragged into things in this rotten way. But, honestly, I've done nothing wrong, and neither has Mark. Nothing that the majority of caring people would think was wrong, anyway. But, of course, the law isn't always on the side of people who want to help others, genuinely help when no one else can or will.'

'Zoe, you've lost me. I don't understand what you're on about.'

'Sorry, sorry! I suppose I'm just trying to convince myself, really, by talking it through – convince myself that it wasn't a crime of any sort. OK, Adam, I'll tell you everything.' She hesitated, took a deep breath and then went on in clinical fashion: 'One of our old ladies, Mrs Lancaster, had been ill for a long time, ill with the sort of problem that couldn't be solved by surgery or anything else. She was dying. Really she should have been in a hospice but she didn't want that, didn't want to be with other terminally sick people. She loved the Villas. She really was a sweetie, never made any fuss, always tried to be cheerful and cheer other people up! I still miss her, you know, and that's the truth.'

Zoe paused again but Adam made no attempt to say anything; he could tell what an effort it was for his sister to talk in this way.

'Well, when the pain and the discomfort got too much

for her, she asked us to give her something that would end it all. She said she wanted to die with dignity. A lot of old people want that almost more than anything, Adam. It matters so much to them. She asked Mark and me because we were the closest ones to her. She hasn't – hadn't – any family. Of course, at first we felt we couldn't possibly do anything like that. For a start, it seems unethical. A hospital – and we are a sort of hospital – is supposed to do its very best to keep people alive, not kill them off. But Mrs Lancaster was dying, anyway. She really couldn't last much longer. And the pain would only have got worse. We would be doing her a kindness. That's the truth. What's more, it's what she wanted. Mark felt we ought to abide by her wishes. Why should she be kept alive for our sakes? If you think about it, Adam, it makes sense.'

He nodded, his own worries temporarily forgotten. Zoe was saying nothing that he could possibly disagree with; she was simply saying how much she cared for someone else's quality of life.

He put his hand over hers. 'I understand, Zoe, and I'm on your side. Go on.'

'When we decided we definitely would do it, Mark wanted to make sure there could be no comeback, no risk of any legal action if it was discovered. So he asked Mrs Lancaster to write a letter, explaining what she wanted and that we were 'helping' her at her request. He felt that would cover us. Foolproof, really. Then we gave her something so that she wouldn't wake up again.'

Zoe ran her tongue along her lips and twirled the ring on her little finger. Adam had questions to ask but she answered the first one before he could say anything.

'We honestly didn't know that she had money, quite a lot of money, really. She left some to the Villas for new medical equipment. And she left some to Mark and to me. But, Adam, you've got to believe me, we truly didn't do it for the money.'

For a moment he wasn't sure that he entirely believed her, but that thought quickly vanished; in the past she had always been transparently honest in everything that had touched them as brother and sister. 'Is that how this guy who's phoned me got to know about it, then? Through the money?'

She shook her head. 'I really don't think so. Bequests to people who work in old folks' homes are not all that unusual. Quite often the patients don't have anyone else close to them to leave it to. And they want to show their gratitude for the care – and love – they've received.'

'So how did it get out, then? The Capri Gang – that's how I think of them because that's the kind of car they drove at me – they must have some proof of what happened, mustn't they? Otherwise how could they blackmail me?'

Zoe pushed her hand through her waves of hair and seemed to be studying the roof of her car. Then she focused on him again. 'I think they must have proof, or what could be regarded as proof. You see, they must have the letter Mrs Lancaster wrote asking us to help her die. If the police saw that and got a court order for an exhumation – you know, have the body dug up – well, I suppose an autopsy would show that death wasn't entirely natural. I don't really know that but I can see it's a possibility. Then they would have to decide who was responsible and ... oh God, it would be awful! It'd be the end of everything.'

'But how could they have got hold of that letter,

Zoe? I mean, surely there aren't any copies?'

She sighed again. 'We didn't know we hadn't got it until you told me about the phone call. Mark put it in the safe, his private safe with other important papers. But when he looked for it this week it wasn't there. Somebody's taken it.'

'But how could they? Surely the safe's kept locked?'

'Of course it is! Most of the time. But in a busy place like ours you can't watch everything that goes on all the time, not even in your own office. There are emergencies and you have to dash off and deal with them, whatever else you might be doing at the time. So it's quite easy to forget to lock your safe if you've been getting something from it and you're desperately needed at the other end of the building. That's what life's like in a nursing home.'

'But who could have taken it?' Adam demanded. 'D'you have any idea?'

Zoe sighed. 'We think so – unfortunately. Or, at least, we can make a good guess. One of our colleagues, a man called John Grievson, well, he's been having money troubles, we know. Once he tried to borrow from Mark, quite a lot of money, actually. Claimed he was in debt but would be able to pay it back in a month. Putting two and two together it sounded as though he'd been losing heavily on gambling. Well, Mark couldn't help and then we heard John was asking for a big pay rise. He didn't get it and we, Mark and I, both thought he was looking a bit desperate. Even his suits were looking tatty. Normally he took such pride in his appearance: always wore a striped tie and a smart blue trilby.' She broke off. 'Adam, what is it?'

He looked as if he'd seen a ghost and, in a sense, he had. 'Oh no!' he exclaimed. 'It must be him, then, the guy who talked to me when I was having a kick around with a couple of kids. Then he turned up immediately after I'd been nearly killed by the Capri. Zoe, he must have watched what happened to me, perhaps even helped to set it up!'

'I'm not with you in all this. Can you explain again?' Zoe looked puzzled.

So Adam told her in detail about his encounters with Blue Hat. He guessed now that he could have been the mystery telephone caller at the training ground. She asked him to describe the man as fully as possible.

'Well, you must be right,' she agreed. 'That sounds exactly like John Grievson. Mark and I are convinced he was the one who rifled the safe and came up with the fatal letter. There's no other likely candidate. It all fits, just as you say.'

'We've got to tackle him, then,' Adam said eagerly. 'Go for him right away and sort it out. Force him to hand over the letter.'

Zoe was shaking her head. 'If only we could! But John's vanished. Mark tried to find him yesterday but he's gone without a trace. He's a bachelor and his landlady says he just cleared off, taking all his clothes and stuff with him. And, surprise, surprise, he owes her money, too. Mark and I suspect John probably sold the letter to some crooks, or perhaps they took it in part-payment of the debt he owes them. Either way, we're powerless. We don't know who the real blackmailers are. Don't suppose we ever will unless John Grievson resurfaces and confesses. But that gang who attacked you sound like professionals, professional criminals.'

Adam slumped in his seat. He felt totally defeated. 'Can't you think of any way we can find out who they are and stop them?' he asked despairingly.

She shook her head and then leaned across to put an arm round his shoulders. 'Our only hope is for you to do exactly what they want. Then they've no reason to bother us any more.'

'But –'

'You've got to help us, Adam, you've got to! Otherwise . . .'

She couldn't finish the sentence. And, at that moment, Adam couldn't think of anything to say that would comfort her or himself.

Ten

With his fingers drumming on the window-ledge, Adam
stared blindly out of the window of the coach at all
the activity on the River Schelde, the ponderous movement of barges and ships and the scurrying of smaller
boats. He just wished they could get to the stadium
and get the match over with as soon as possible. Then
his ordeal would end and perhaps he could start to
live again.

'Never realised this place was such a big port, you
know,' Karl Holliday remarked to him as the bus
turned away from the waterfront and edged past some
impressive Gothic buildings. 'The only place I'd really
heard of in Belgium is Brussels. And that's only
because they're supposed to grow the best sprouts
there!'

'Don't you know anything, Hollers?' Ricky Gannon
asked in mock disbelief. Ricky had the ability to overhear any conversation however far away he was; and
as he was in the seat directly behind Adam and Karl
he couldn't miss anything they said. 'This is one of
the big ports of the world as well as a centre of the
diamond industry. You ought to learn something useful
instead of frittering your time away on racing and ten-
pin bowling and that sort of rubbish . . . then you could

put your money to some use instead of chucking it away.'

'Easy come, easy go, live today, not tomorrow, that's my style, Ritzy, old mate,' Karl replied chirpily. 'When I get my win bonus for scoring the goals that beat the old Belgians tonight I'll enjoy spending it. I don't want to stick my head into the financial papers like you to see how to invest it. That sort of attitude takes all the pleasure, all the fun, out of living.'

'Don't bank on that bonus, Hollers,' the central defender warned him. 'I read the tabloids as well, you know, and one of them mentions that there's been heavy betting on RSV to win this match. *Unusually* heavy betting, it says. 'Course that couldn't happen in England, you know. Bookmakers won't take bets on just a single match. So maybe somebody knows something we don't – like RSV being a better outfit than Ouch says they are.'

'That's just newspaper talk,' Karl scoffed. 'They'll write anything to whip up a bit of interest in a Cup match abroad. The reporter just wants to make sure his Sports Editor sends him out to cover the game. Thought you'd know that, Ritzy.'

Adam leaned back in his seat, eyes closed. So that was it! He was being ordered to throw the match so that the Capri Gang could make a financial killing. That was the conclusion he and Zoe had come to after talking about the probable motive. At first, Adam had supposed the Gang had some connection with the Antwerp club and just wanted to ensure that the team reached the next round, so guaranteeing further income for everyone. But that seemed unlikely. Top clubs didn't go in for bribery. It was too risky. It was a different matter, however, for an individual who was able to organise a betting success by blackmailing a goalkeeper. Unless he deliberately identified himself, the blackmailer would remain anonymous. His plot to get what he wanted was just about foolproof so long as his victim obeyed orders.

'Skips, you OK?' Karl inquired. 'Never known you so quiet. Not suffering from something, are you?' He lowered his voice. 'I mean, it happens. We all claim we're fit when we're not, we all turn out when we shouldn't just so somebody else won't grab our place and play too damned well!'

Adam opened his eyes and tried to smile. He'd been given an easy excuse for his silence. 'I'm OK, really. Just didn't enjoy the flight too much. Flying always seems to upset my system a bit. But I'll be fine by the time the game starts.'

'Understood,' Karl nodded sympathetically. 'Known quite a few players who've never fancied flying, actually. Still, just as long as you're fit to celebrate our win tonight. I hear the night-life in Brussels is sensational.'

Adam smiled because he had to show some reaction. But he knew that when they returned to their hotel in the capital he'd just want to go to bed and blot out the horrors of the match.

Ian Fenn was sure his young goalkeeper was going to have a marvellous game: and he said as much when the players strolled on to the pitch to admire the setting, immediately after they'd arrived at the modern stadium on the edge of the city.

'Doesn't that inspire you, Adam?' he asked, pointing to the towering, two-tier cantilever stand. 'All those spectators up there, just dying to see great goals and great saves? OK, I know we're not Brazil or Barcelona or Bayern Munich. But, if we're on our top form tonight, we could still have 'em jumping out of their seats, cheering our brilliance. We want to give 'em a night to remember!'

'Looks great, Boss,' agreed Adam, beginning to wonder why he was being singled out for this display of enthusiasm. 'I just hope we live up to your expectations.'

He knew that sounded fatuous but didn't know what else to say. Could Ian Fenn somehow have heard that his goalkeeper might throw the match? Was this a warning? Impossible! The Boss couldn't know. If he'd heard even the faintest whisper then Adam would have been removed from the squad immediately. He wouldn't have been allowed within a hundred miles of the RSV Stadium, Antwerp. No, there was nothing suspicious about Ian Fenn's remarks: the Manager was simply on a football high, chasing Cup glory for once, not bread-and-butter League points.

'Look, son, just one thing I want to say,' Ian Fenn continued. 'You had a bad game against Watford, in spite of that penalty save. That was about the only thing you did that was real quality. I know you didn't play well, you know you didn't. But you've got that bad game out of your system. Tonight, the Watford performance doesn't matter a damn. You're guarding our goal because I think you're the best keeper we've got. If I didn't think that, I'd've put Jake between the posts. After all, I've brought him here with us. But tonight you'll be in prime form again, I'm sure of it. So don't let me down, OK?'

'OK, Boss.'

To Adam's surprise, Rob Heanor had very little to say to him when the players trooped into the changing-room just over half an hour before the kick-off. Much of the coach's time seemed to be taken up with discussing defensive ploys with Ricky, Sim Rokefield and Glen

Quartley. It was Glen's first away match in the first team and he was looking just a little nervous. Rob was drumming into him the need to keep RSV's speedy German winger out on the touchline. 'When he cuts inside and is given an inch of space he's twice as dangerous,' Rob reiterated. 'I told you, he can hit 'em hard with either foot so you never know just when he's going to shoot. So, Glen, son, clamp down on him, keep him out on the wide horizon.'

At the team talk and pre-match analysis the day before, Adam had been given much the same message about the winger's sharp-shooting and his unexpected change of pace. As Ricky himself had remarked many times, the management never believed in telling you anything once, only a dozen times. They seemed to believe that none of their players was intelligent enough to take anything in the first time. Yet, if you heard something too many times you got bored with it, even forgot it. But Ricky couldn't convince Rob of that.

Adam, too, was listening to Ouch in case something more was said about the RSV striker who'd be wearing the No. 9 shirt, the player who would take any penalty kick awarded to his team. It was only the previous day he'd learned he was actually an Englishman, Daniel Hastie, who'd been discovered by the Belgian club while playing in the south of England in the Beazer Homes League, which proved what a remarkable international scouting system RSV possessed. 'Highly mobile, likely to turn up anywhere, any time – the all-action man, he is,' was Rob Heanor's description of Hastie.

Adam had no way of knowing whether Hastie was part of the plot; it was perfectly possible the Capri Gang simply knew that the RSV striker always hit penalty kicks to the left of the keeper. Therefore, if RSV won such a kick and Hastie took it he would be sure to score if Adam went the other way. Still, all that seemed too speculative for a gang so well organised in every other respect.

'OK, son, feeling good?' Rob inquired jocularly as he passed Adam on his way to confer with his manager for the last time before the game began. Adam automatically nodded. 'Have a good game, then, son. Have a good game.'

For once, every player, apart from himself, seemed completely relaxed and eager to get on with the game. Even Glen appeared to have put his earlier worries about trying to subdue the German flying ace behind him. The novelty of playing abroad – and for City it really was a novelty as they hadn't qualified for a European competition for a very long time – had plainly affected their attitude. The home supporters wouldn't know what to expect of them and so City wanted to put on a show to impress them. The players were keen to win a reputation that would put them on a par with Arsenal and Manchester United and Liverpool, Rangers and Celtic and Aberdeen, as a top British team.

They ran out to some very polite applause from what looked, at first glance, to be a fairly sparse attendance. But it was such a huge stadium that even a moderately good crowd might appear lost in it. To their delight, a sizeable party of City supporters had made the trip and were congregated behind one of the goals, waving Union Jacks and scarves in the club's colours of blue-and-white. Clapping with their hands held high above their heads, the City players jogged across towards that enclosure to show their appreciation of the support they were getting.

'Makes you want to win tonight just for them, doesn't it?' remarked Karl, who seemed genuinely affected by the sight of their fans on foreign soil.

'Yeah, it sure does,' Adam replied because he had to say something. But Karl's comment was another twist of the knife in his stomach.

RSV emerged to the sound of firecrackers and whistles and hooters, sounds altogether different from those at a Football League ground. Theirs was an unusual strip in brown-and-yellow with scarlet trim and they presented a colourful spectacle as the entire team performed the local equivalent of a war dance in the centre circle before the officials trotted out on to the pitch to share in the exchange of handshakes and pennants and club plaques. Adam, who'd been fielding shots in the goalmouth from his team-mates, as he always did before the start of a match, was surprised to be summoned to the middle to meet not only the referee and linesmen but the RSV goalkeeper as well; it was all part of the plan to promote as friendly an atmosphere as possible for the match.

Even Rob Heanor got on to the pitch for an unaccustomed greeting and he took the opportunity of having a last word with one or two of his players, including Adam. 'Don't forget, concentrate – concentrate like a man conducting an orchestra!' It was an unlikely simile for him and Adam didn't know where the coach had picked it up, but it wasn't the first time he'd used it. Concentration was a subject he never let up on.

Ricky Gannon was revelling in his role as captain on this occasion and there wasn't any doubt he'd hang on to the pennant he received from the RSV skipper. As the teams lined up for the kick-off, Ricky made a point of signalling his determination to win to every one of his co-defenders: his clenched fist was also a warning to them not to make any errors.

Predictably, RSV surged into the attack from the outset and Hastie fed the German winger, Doernberg, with a measured pass. Darren Marsh, one of City's midfielders, had already moved across in anticipation of such a move but he was unable to intercept the ball. With Glen Quartley soon back-pedalling and Doernberg moving the ball along with obvious confidence, the home crowd began to bay for a goal. Would the winger cut in and shoot or take the ball down to the dead ball line before centering? As his defence funnelled back, Adam jinked up and down on his line, ready to make a decisive interception or catch.

Then, with a sudden change of pace and little more than a shake of his hips, the winger rounded Glen and turned inside; but instead of continuing his run he unexpectedly hit a low cross to a team-mate on the opposite flank; and he, in turn, hooked the ball into the penalty area, aiming for Daniel Hastie. Hastie, running in diagonally, struck on the volley, sending the ball flashing across the face of the goal and grazing the far upright as it went out of play. It had been a close thing and the fans gave their attackers a rapturous reception as they moved back upfield.

If only that ball had gone into the net, Adam reflected, then RSV would have been one up and no one could have blamed him for letting in the goal. City's players would have been deflated at the very start of the match and would have found it difficult to win from that point. His problem might well have been solved without his having to take any sort of action himself.

Still, the Belgian side was clearly talented and they'd surely create other openings before long. In fact, City seemed to take heart from that let-off: or, at least, some of the players did. Darren Marsh, tackling with great zest, emerged from a mêlée in the centre circle with the ball at his feet: and was obviously determined to keep it there. His dribble past two defenders was a revelation and it carried him to the very edge of the penalty area where, after exchanging a smart one-two with Ian Fenn, he was unable to resist the temptation to try a shot at goal. It would have gone in, too, if the goalie hadn't managed to get a hand to it and turn the ball over the bar. City's supporters, located behind the goal, cheered vociferously.

Ian, patting his young colleague on the back, took the corner himself, swinging the ball in to the near post where Karl was stationed to flick his header into the goalmouth; and Ricky Gannon, on cue, powered in to head the ball before any defender could reach it. But, like Hastie at the other end, his aim was fractionally off target and the ball skimmed over the bar. Ricky looked furious with himself but he had no need to: he'd convinced RSV and their supporters that City were a clever, attacking side. Ricky took a few congratulatory calls from team-mates as he returned to the defence, and one of them was from Adam, if only for appearances' sake. In truth, Adam's eyes had rolled upwards in some relief when the ball went over the bar instead of under it.

For the next few minutes, play was confined almost entirely to the middle third of the pitch as each side strove to establish supremacy. No one was working harder than Darren Marsh, tackling heroically, distributing skilfully and economically and running powerfully whenever he glimpsed an opening. Rob Heanor had given him the specific task of clamping down on Daniel Hastie: and, since that early moment when he'd got in a shot at goal, the former English non-League player had led a very restricted life.

City seemed to be getting on top. RSV had been pinned in their own half for some time when, more in desperation than anything else, a defender slammed the ball as hard as he could upfield. Hastie, reacting with his usual speed, darted past his marker and chased after it. A couple of City defenders instantly claimed offside but the linesman's flag stayed by his side as he matched strides with Hastie on a parallel course. City had pushed up so far that Adam now had that half of the pitch to himself – apart from the on-rushing Antwerp striker.

He responded to the situation instinctively. All calculations went out of his head. His only thought was to prevent RSV scoring a simple goal. If Hastie reached the ball before he did then all it would need was a body swerve and a cool nerve: in that situation, so far out of his penalty area, Adam couldn't use his hands. If he did he would be committing what was regarded as a professional foul.

Adam's sprint, allied to his determination, took him to the ball no more than a second ahead of his opponent. It wasn't possible to direct his kick anywhere. All he could manage was to send the ball as far as possible into the other half of the pitch (it never occurred to him that he had an alternative: to kick it over the touch-line and so out of play. It would hardly have mattered that Antwerp would then have been awarded a throw-in).

His last-ditch clearance brought a delirious response from the visiting fans as well as a wave of appreciation from a relieved Ricky. And, in that moment, Adam knew he'd made the right decision. He'd spent a sleepless night trying to decide what he should do to resolve his dilemma. All his instincts, however, were to play for his team and play as hard as was needed to win. To do anything else would be to lose his own self-respect and to commit professional suicide. Football was his life, a life he loved beyond anything else.

By chance his clearance reached Darren Marsh who made no attempt to trap the ball or take it under control. Instead, from his position on the right flank he simply hammered the ball diagonally across the pitch towards Karl Holliday. With pantherish speed, Karl pounced on the pass, took the ball on for a couple of strides and then unleashed a shot from outside the penalty area before any defender could get close to him.

It was the unexpectedness of the shot as well as its pace and accuracy that defeated the goalkeeper. He hardly saw the ball as it streaked over his left shoulder – he was positioned close to the six-yard line – and lifted the top of the net by the far post. In the colourful prose of one newspaper reporter at the match, the goal was 'as big a surprise as meeting the devil on Christmas morning in your own kitchen!'

Adam, acknowledging the signals of jubilation from Karl and the Boss, began to think he was slowly going mad. Why on earth hadn't he missed the ball when he dashed out of goal? Nothing would have been easier. Goalkeepers weren't expected to perform miracles as outfield players. In a fifty-fifty situation like the one with Daniel Hastie, it was the easiest thing in the world to take your eye off the ball and miskick; it happened all the time at all levels of football. Now he'd not only cleared the danger to his own side, he'd provided an opening which Darren and Karl, between them, had converted into a spectacular goal, a goal that had, literally, shot City into the lead, a goal that would change both the tempo and the temperature of the match. How could he have been so stupid? He continued asking himself that until the first half ended.

Eleven

The rest of the team were still bubbling with excitement as they piled into the changing-room for cups of tea or well-sugared fruit juices. Even Rob Heanor was proclaiming that he couldn't remember a better goal from that distance; and by now Karl himself was trying (unsuccessfully, because it just wasn't his nature) to appear modest about his achievement. 'Just hit it first time, you know, and in it flew!' he explained several times.

'Terrific performance, son, terrific!' was Rob's reaction when he came to sit beside Adam and put his arm round his shoulders. 'You did just right. Shows the value of concentration! What did I tell you!'

Adam smiled his gratitude at his coach: it was true, he had been concentrating so hard on the game that everything else was blotted out of his mind. Now, though, his dilemma resurfaced: how would the Capri Gang react to City's performance and half-time lead? There was no way of telling. In any case, perhaps none of them was there. By the time Adam left home there was still no trace of John (Blue Hat) Grievson. So it looked as though he'd gone for good, much to Zoe's and Mark's relief. Quite possibly Grievson had merely shown the vital letter to the blackmailers instead of handing it over. There was no way Adam or Zoe could tell whether the threat to them was real or empty. But Adam was gambling that nothing would happen if City did win. Of course, if they lost then the problem shouldn't arise.

There was hardly any need for a pep-talk because the team was eager to go out and finish what they'd started. Tradition, though, is hard to overcome in football. So Rob had a few words to say: 'All you've got to do now, is keep playing as you've been playing. You're on top and they know it. Another goal could clinch it for us. They'll come out fighting but we've shown we can repel 'em. No fancy work, no frills, remember, and like the Boss said before the match, shoot on sight! That's a winner, that is.'

He was so pleased with that phrase that he really wanted to repeat it but recently he'd learned that in the emotional atmosphere of a changing-room midway through a vital match, players could only absorb the smallest amount of advice (that was according to a sports psychologist, anyway). So he refrained from saying another word. From what he could see, they'd got the message, anyway.

Most spectators had been predicting during the interval that RSV would come out in the second half like a fire brigade, eager to put out the flames and restore things to normal. But they seemed subdued and it was City who launched the first attack. They believed a second goal would win the tie for them. But the movement came to naught when, for once, Darren Marsh lost the ball in a tackle by Hastie, who seemed to be dropping ever deeper into his own half of the field. Then, as Darren attempted to regain control, Hastie collapsed, clasping his right knee and clearly in pain.

Inevitably, Darren got a talking to by the referee although the tackle had been quite fair. So far the game had been played in a good spirit and this was the first time a trainer had been on to the pitch to attend to an injury. No one had been booked for any offence and there'd been no sign of anger anywhere.

It was some moments before Daniel Hastie felt well enough to resume and even then he seemed to suffer with each move. Adam now had something else to worry about. If the Number 9 didn't take any penalty that was awarded, who would? But that matter, too, went out of his mind a minute later when RSV at last got the ball out to Doernberg. His approach, this time, was of the slow, slow, slow, quick variety as he appeared intent on mesmerising Glen Quartley. Even RSV's own supporters weren't enamoured of this style of play: they sensed that time wasn't on their side. So they yelled at the German to get going or to get rid of the ball. Because he was an artist, he managed to do both at the same time. His trick was to flick the ball against Glen's shins and then snap up the rebound while accelerating past City's left-back. Glen, annoyed at being outwitted in that way, lunged at his opponent but was far too late to make any contact. Now there was a gap in City's defence and the German winger arrowed towards the penalty area.

Adam hopped up and down on his line, trying to work out what Doernberg would do with the ball. Ricky was yelling to Simon Rokefield to watch RSV's left-winger: but the advice came a split-second too late. As if recalling how City scored their goal with the aid of a cross-field pass, the German suddenly hammered the ball towards the other side of the box where his opposite number, reaching it centimetres ahead of Simon, headed it hard into the goalmouth.

It was Ricky who managed to get his head to the ball, but not very effectively because he was off-balance. The ball looped away to his right where Daniel Hastie had arrived. As it dropped Hastie had his back to the goal but that was no problem to him. Falling backwards, he met the ball perfectly in mid-air with a bicycle kick. Because, of course, he couldn't see where to aim, it was his natural goal-scorer's instinct that directed his shot into the top right-hand corner of the net past a transfixed and astounded Adam Skipsea.

The ground erupted as the home fans rose to acclaim another breath-taking goal – this time for their own team. The cheering and the firecrackers and the clapping were still filling the air as City kicked off again. Adam was still shaking his head and there was nothing artificial about his reaction. An overhead kick in a crowded penalty-area invariably produces a shot that the goalkeeper hasn't a chance of anticipating: it really could go anywhere. Hastie's deadly shot was quite definitely the best he'd ever seen (or, to be strictly accurate, not seen until the ball entered the net). No blame could possibly be attached to him for failing to stop it. Even England's current goalkeeper would have been defeated by it. Ricky, who felt that he was the one at fault for not clearing the ball with his header, had simply shrugged when he and Adam exchanged glances after the goal was scored. The defence could console themselves with the thought that it had taken a goal of stupendous artistry to beat them.

Inevitably, after such a fillip, the Belgian team sensed that victory would soon be theirs. His goal appeared to have restored Daniel Hastie to full fitness (in fact, he hadn't been as badly hurt as he made out and it was his undiminished pace that had enabled him to get into the City box in time for his shot). Instead of hovering around RSV's part of the centre circle, he moved forward to join in any attack that developed. His transfer to RSV had given his career a new lease of life; now his sights were set on gilding it with a Cup-winners' medal.

Darren, who blamed himself for allowing Hastie to reach the ball in the penalty area, resumed his close-marking role. Whichever way the English-born striker turned, Marsh was sure to follow. Twice, Hastie, determined to avoid another crunching tackle from his shadow, allowed the ball intended for him to pass on to someone else by skipping over it. Darren, however, was not going to be outwitted by subtleties of that nature. In his book, Hastie was a match-winner and so had to be prevented from getting in sight of his goal with the ball at his feet.

Adam was soon in action again, catching two high centres, one from either wing, and he was quick to throw the ball out to a team-mate so as to waste no time at all. The minutes were ticking away and constantly his eyes turned to the huge clock, its numerals composed of the letters of an advertiser's name. A re-play in England would be torment for him but at least City might have a better chance to win on home ground. Of course, a replay was the last thing the Capri Gang would want. Unusually, this wasn't a competition with home-and-away legs, which was another reason why RSV themselves were so anxious to score again.

Karl had been largely subdued since scoring his goal by the astute marking of RSV's speediest defender and now Ian Fenn switched his wingers. The move paid off at once with an incisive run by Karl that took him into the penalty area: where he was scythed down by the other full-back. Practically the entire City team appealed for a penalty and, for a moment, it seemed that the referee would reward them. But then, without even consulting a linesman, he waved play on. Adam groaned: a penalty for City then would surely have settled the issue.

Two minutes later it was the home supporters who had something to shout about. This time, when he received a pass from Doernberg, Daniel Hastie retained possession and attempted to jink past his marker. He almost succeeded. Then, desperately, Darren lunged with all his weight: and both players crashed to the turf. Darren was the only one to get up and instantly started to protest his innocence. The referee, reaching for notebook, pencil and card, took in at a glance the injury to the Belgian player and summoned medical help. The boos and hisses and whistling from the fans were prolonged as Darren received his caution; and the interruption to play was added to by the time it took for the RSV officials to carry off their injured hero and send on a substitute. Ian Fenn wasn't the only member of the City team to believe that Darren was lucky not to be sent off for his offence: Darren himself thought so. Still, although not with deliberate intent, he had disposed of RSV's most dangerous striker.

Worriedly, Adam pushed his fingers through his hair. He'd known where to dive if Hastie took a penalty. But where would a replacement kicker aim? Adam mentally crossed his fingers and hoped that he'd guess right.

The Number 12 was tall and blond-haired and his first touch of the ball was a flick-on for Doernberg to chase, control and then return to him on the edge of the area. Adam instinctively advanced. RSV's substitute, seeing the keeper off his line, instantaneously tried to lob him. To disappointed 'oooo-oh's' from the crowd, the ball landed on the crossbar and bounced out of play.

'Close one, that, Skips. So watch it!' Ricky warned him anxiously.

Adam took his time collecting the ball from a ball-boy. After a scare, it was always best to slow things down. Now, with time running out, Ian Fenn ordered his wingers to drop back to bolster City's defence. It was, as he admitted later, an unwise move; but he'd been thinking about a replay at home in front of a large crowd willing to pay higher prices to see City overcome an attractive foreign team.

Urged on by his manager, who had been gesticulating towards the clock and could no longer remain seated on the bench, Doernberg drew on his last reserves of energy when one of his team-mates hit a long ball out of defence towards him. Again, his sorcery accounted for Glen, though in fairness to City's left-back he was now so tired he ought to have been replaced. The German winger changed direction twice as other opponents challenged him. Then, just when it seemed he would go all the way to goal on his own, he suddenly scooped the ball towards the blond substitute who was charging headlong towards the goal-mouth. Ricky Gannon, seeing what was about to happen and believing that a goal was inevitable from such short range, flung himself sideways in his effort to intercept the ball – and flattened the Number 12.

There wasn't a soul in the stadium who thought it wasn't a penalty.

Adam moistened his lips. Who was going to take the crucial penalty? Nobody had picked up the ball in proprietorial fashion, wiped it on his shirt and then, with studied care, placed on the spot. RSV's substitute was receiving attention from their physio and so it seemed he would be the taker if he recovered from his knock. Would he follow Hastie's intention and shoot for the bottom corner to Adam's left? If so, he wouldn't score – because Adam was determined to frustrate him in the same way as he would have frustrated Hastie.

As soon as the substitute stood up and indicated that he was fit enough to carry on, Ricky Gannon darted up to Adam. 'No idea where this one'll aim for,' he muttered. 'Just do your best, Skips. Good luck. Sorry I let you in for this.'

A hush enveloped the stadium as the kicker placed the ball, retreated two or three metres, paused, and then ran at the ball. Adam, having spotted the kicker's split-second glance to his right, was already moving as the ball flashed towards the foot of his left-hand post. It struck that post, on the outside, and went out of play.

The collective gasp from the crowd was almost deafening after that temporary silence. Adam, picking himself up, experienced a surge of relief. His nightmare was over! The penalty had been missed anyway!

In the midst of all the expressions of amazement or horror or delight, few of the players realised that the referee was again pointing to the spot while waiting for the ball to be returned to him. And it was a moment or two longer before Adam grasped the fact that he was going to have to face another kick because he'd committed the cardinal sin of moving before the first kick was taken. So City might still lose if the Belgian substitute could shoot more accurately this time.

But where would he aim this time? Having missed one target, would he now choose another? If he did, then the odds would surely favour the bottom right-hand corner. Adam focused on the man's eyes. If there was a clue, they would supply it. As the Belgian moved back to begin his run-up Adam just had time to decide that, whatever else, he mustn't move before boot struck ball.

Even if he had moved prematurely, it's doubtful whether he could have saved the shot. For the ball, struck with tremendous power, rocketed past him to make the net bulge above his right shoulder. Adam's flailing arms made no contact with it at all. The goal-scorer disappeared in the deluge of delight displayed by his team-mates.

Adam, after retrieving the ball and punting it upfield, sank on his haunches. Now the worst really was over – in one sense. He'd played for his team, he'd saved them when the odds were stacked against them, and yet, by sheer irony, the blackmailers had got the result they wanted, if they still wanted it. Zoe no longer had anything to worry about. The losers were City – but they hadn't lost because of his actions.

For, with less than a minute's play remaining, there really wasn't time for City to save the game, though they still managed to stage a frenzied finish with one shot on target from Ian Fenn, which was faultlessly held by the keeper.

When the final whistle shrilled, Ian made a point of coming across to have a word with his young goal-keeper.

'Don't worry about that penalty, son,' the Manager said with a wan grin. 'No blame's attached to you. Just wasn't our lucky night. I mean, what can you say when a guy misses a penalty and then has a second chance!'

'All my fault, I knocked the bloke over,' confessed Ricky, coming up to join them as they entered the tunnel. 'Never given away a penalty like that in my life!'

115

The manager put his arm on Ricky's shoulders. 'Forget it, Ricky. Football's always been like that. Some you're lucky to win, some you're unlucky to lose. Tonight was one of the unlucky ones. What matters is the next match – and making sure we win it. Then the world will look bright again.'

Secretly, Adam was exultant already. For he felt he'd not only defied criminals but actually defeated an enemy, an enemy that was faceless but still as real to him as a player taking a penalty kick against him. It was really like winning a European Cup-tie on his own.

One day, that's exactly what Adam Skipsea would do as City's goalkeeper.

Also by Michael Hardcastle

SOCCER CAPTAIN

Fast-paced footballing action in the world of the
Sunday League

It's a disastrous season for the Hurlford Hawks. As
they sink further and further into the depths of the
League even their coach gives up and deserts them.
Could this be the end of the line for the heroic
Hawks?

Just as they are about to give up hope, Lynda Hes-
keth steps in as their new coach. She's a woman with
strong ideas on training, and plans to take her new
team to the top. But can she succeed where a man has
failed?

There are a few surprises in store . . . particularly
when Lynda chooses the most unpredictable player as
captain.

1 85881 071 X   £3.99

ONE GOOD HORSE

Puzzle is a horse who lives up to his name

As soon as she sees him, Holly knows there's something special about this horse. He has the look of a
conqueror, a winner. But the trouble with Puzzle is
that he is unpredictable and volatile, in need of careful handling and training.

It's just the job for Holly's father, an experienced
racehorse trainer who's down on his luck. Could
Puzzle be the one good horse Holly and her dad need
to make their mark?

1 85881 106 6   £3.99